# Night Flights

### Original Prose and Poetry from Brighton NightWriters 2015

Published in Great Britain 2015 by Brighton NightWriters

Editor: Rosemary Allix

Cover artwork and Design: Fayjay

Copyright by the authors, all rights reserved

ISBN: 978-1515299219

Printed by: Create Space

Brighton NightWriters have been meeting once a week to discuss each other's work in a friendly, supportive atmosphere for over 25 years. Some of us have been going along since the beginning, some are complete newcomers, some attend regularly, some irregularly.

NightWriters meets upstairs at a pub in the Queens Park area of Brighton every Wednesday at 7.30pm.

New writers are always welcome. Just come along or contact Tim Shelton-Jones on 01273 505642 for more information.

Visit our website at: www.nightwriters.org.uk

# CONTENTS

# Aidan Hopkins

*I am a middle-aged financial translator living in Hollingdean, Brighton. Mostly I write light short stories with a slightly weird tone. This is not deliberate. It is just the way they come out. Sometimes I worry about this*

# The Sugar House

### *Hallowe'en*

"Go on!" hissed his brother, one of a gang of ghouls and zombies milling safely on the street side of the gate. Zak was unclear how it had come down to him. John Boyle had started picking on people, half-scrapping with Martin McNally before turning on Zak's big brother, who claimed he'd done it before, and somehow this had meant it came down to Zak, who was now standing alone just inside the gate of the witch house.

No-one trick-or-treated here. Shiny bushes overhung the path, near black in the orange streetlight. At the end, the house reared up dark and jagged against the half-lit clouds, its lines confused by whispering bare branches. There was nothing to be scared of, he thought. Witches were unreal, an adult invention to liven up parties. He was much more terrified of John Boyle, he thought, and realised for the first time that he might actually be going to do this.

The house was not much odder than others in the street, just a bit run-down with brown ragged lace curtains that no-one ever changed in the downstairs windows. Spiders for sure. A big once-gold knocker hung flaking on the door. He took a step forward and felt a tight electric hush fall on the boys behind him. Two more paces and he was suddenly half-way. Nothing moved. OK, he thought, OK, and summoning all his nine-year-old swiftness launched himself toward the knocker, seized the cold heavy thing in his hand and slammed it down hard three times with a startling flat Blatt Blatt Blatt. Then, mad with daring he bent down, jerked open the letter box and shouted "Witch, witch, little witch". He glanced back at the hysterical group at the gate and saw they had had enough. His brother was waving madly that he should get the hell out. John Boyle was already slipping off. But his nerve held one moment more, just long enough to look back and see, behind the downstairs window not a yard away, a round face that stared out once and vanished, leaving only the net curtain swinging dustily behind him as he fled.

## Guy Fawkes Night

Inquisitions followed and under another saddening November sky Zak was led back, his mother steering Katy's pushchair with one hand and pulling Zak along with the other. The opposite of fun.

This time, the house seemed less scary but gloomier. Zak edged back as she marched unflinchingly up to the door and knocked. Silence. Seconds ticked by and he had just started to hope when, from deep within, there came a scraping sound, like a kitchen chair dragged across tiles, moving nearer. It reached the door and paused. Zak held his breath. Then with the rattle of a chain, the door swung painfully open and low down, near flush with Zak's head, the witch poked out her long nose. She was stooped over her walking frame and all in black. The left side of her face hung slack and dead but her right eye glinted bright with malice. The mouth was clamped shut amid a nest of hairs and wrinkles. When his mother spoke the normality of her voice made him jump.

"Sorry to bother you. This is my son Zachary, and he has something he wants to say, about the other night." She squeezed his hand hard as the witch's eye swung onto him.

"Sorry to bother you," he managed, trying to rally his thoughts. "Err. I'm sorry. On Halloween I banged on your door. It was a kind of joke. I'm sorry." Phew. That was it, please God.

His words hung in the air so long he thought she must be stupid. In the silence Katy started to burble and his mother bent down.

But when it came, the witch's voice was soft and somehow stilted, as though she had learnt to speak from a film.

"What is your name, boy?"

"Zak." He offered, recoiling.

"Zak," she said, taking his name in her mouth.

"I'm sorry," he said again, hoping to put an end to this.

But the live half of the woman's face twisted suddenly into a smile.

"Not to worry," she said, and to his horror beckoned him in "Come, come," and hitched her rackety frame around. His mother looked at him once and let his hand go.

No help there.

He stepped over the threshold.

Inside, the hall floor was tiled in geometric patterns vanishing under drifts of grit. The wallpaper looked furry and had perhaps once had red flowery patterns, now darkened and given a greasy cast by the yellow light of the one old-fashioned bulb that hung from the ceiling half-way down. Beyond, all was dim.

The witch wobbled ahead in the sickly light and reluctantly, he followed. Once again, just two fidgety steps seemed to take him deep in. They pressed on slowly, past the bulb and now he could see they were heading for an open door at the end of the hall, toward what seemed to be a kitchen. Something inside him wanted to laugh.

"Come, come" said the witch again, scraping ahead. Glancing back, Zak could still see his mother and Katy framed in the outside air, but they looked small and elsewhere.

He took a last step and was in the kitchen, or rather a mockery of what had once been a kitchen. A grimly functional microwave took pride of place. The cooker seemed neglected and desolate, while all around lay the ghastly plastic accoutrements of old age. Strange-shaped vessels kept handy. Grip bars and little wheels on otherwise normal furnishings. The only wholesome thing he saw was a huge copper pot that hung shining above the fireplace looking proud and lost, as though it didn't belong in this shrunken little space.

And then he saw the sugar house, standing on the table. The roof was made of gingerbread and the snow of icing sugar. From the chocolate chimney smoke curled. It was clearly meant to be a big house but not a mansion, nor quite like any house he had ever seen before, with white walls, a big bay window on the ground floor criss-crossed with what looked like twiglets and a green door hung on real hinges, its gold handle garnished, with miniature care, by a wreath of tiny green holly leaves, the red berries no bigger than pinheads. As he stared the witch's head loomed up by his shoulder.

"The sugar house," she murmured. "A pretty thing, yes? It is very old. Really, you should see it in gaslight." She inched her way around again and fumbled some matches out of a drawer. Then, with a sigh, she bent down and turned her attention to the ancient oven.

Zak was still looking at the sugar house. He extended his skinny finger and as delicately as he could gave the door a tiny push. It did not give, but, to his horror, his nail brushed the wreath which dropped to the table. Panicking, he thought to stick it back on and picking up the tiny thing with his pinky he tried to moisten it with his tongue. Bad move. The exquisite leaves evaporated on contact in a sudden waft of dusty sweetness and other flavours which might have been cloves and cinnamon.

A rush of warmth ran up his back and he looked round. The witch had lit the oven and was watching him calmly.

"Now, that's better," she said. "Look at the windows " and she tugged on a cord. The electric light went out with a pop.

In the querulous gaslight the sugar house seemed to leap into life. The windows of spun sugar became blurry, translucent and layered. Behind the big bay window lace curtains seemed to shift and waver. And behind them shadows were forming, shapes, as of men and women moving in the pale blue flickering light. The aged oven coughed and the shapes shrank back then jumped out, resolving into whirling forms before his eyes, couples stepping in time to unheard music.

"We used to dance," crowed the witch. "We had such waltzes, you would not believe. Do you know what it is to waltz?" He could smell her breath now, she was so close, and her voice was fierce and young.

"Look. Look in the upstairs window" she commanded. His eyes drew upward, away from the dancing shadows, crawling up over the rough icing of the wall, where for the first time, he noticed a delicate tracery of dark ivy encrusted on with clever fingers leading on to the sill and to the bedroom window.

This time the shadows resolved themselves more quickly, perhaps because he had expected to see this: an old, four-poster bed, with woven hangings drifting around and rich coverlets falling to the floor. And lying on the coverlets....was that a princess lying there? No. Not a princess. He peered closer into the mist. There was a shape on the bed, but it was not still. A shadow that moved and writhed and resolved into two and then one. With a start he realised what he was looking at, leapt back and stared at the witch whose was now laughing straight into his face.

"We used to dance," she cackled. "We used to dance." Without a thought in his head he bolted back through the hall and out to his mother and Katy waiting coldly in the free air beyond to take him to the bonfire party.

### *Festival of Saint Vlad, midnight*

Blatt, Blatt, Blatt.

"Who's there?"

Blatt, Blatt, Blatt.

"Don't go."

"Who's there?"

"Who cares?"

"I must go."

"What do we care? What do we care? Stay here."

"It's best to go, Hexchen, just to see."

"Don't go. Stay here. Stay here with me.

# reppilS ssalG

The Collector hated this village. He had cut across country to get here and could feel the soddenness in his socks but he kept his eyes honest as he waited, curious children clustering around his coat tails. Had she heard his knock?

She was a simple, sly old woman of the sort that infested the Bavarian backwoods. The simpleness came with the country. The slyness, he guessed, she had picked up as a girl. If she guessed what he was after she would plonk down her fat arse and make him pay.

"Grüß Gott, mother," he said, when the door opened at last, rolling the gruff dialect syllables in his throat. "Have you got any cakes for me today?"

The old woman didn't answer, but crouched back on her stool by the hearth with its bare mantelpiece, and poked the black grate with its black coals.

"I was in Rome, once," she said. She always began like that, to try and impress he supposed. If true, she had no doubt gone with the army and he could guess what she had been doing.

"I cleaned for the Pope, you know."

He did. She had told him many times. Well she'd still come back to this hole. The Pope couldn't have been that impressed with her cleaning. Her cakes were nothing special either but he wasn't here for the cakes.

"What say we have a smoke?" he offered, as usual, and she turned around and for the first time looked at him straight, "…and a story."

He filled the pipes, got out his notebook, and she began.

"Back there, in a valley where the hills start to climb toward the mountains and where the streams are just wide enough and clear enough for the trout to make their way home…"

From his hiding place in the clothes basket Rufkin heard the traditional opening and the scratching of the pen. He liked it in the linen basket. It gave him a sense of place, a feeling of knowing where you were.

He didn't like the pompous man, with the stiff back and dirty cuffs. A town man who couldn't talk properly and understood nothing, stomping through the trout stream as though it was just another ditch, addressing idiot Joan as "Madame" and trying to pay the mayor's heavy toll with one of his protestant shillings.

Today it was a girl's story and he let his attention wander while it wound to its close and after some to-ing and fro-ing the man with the grubby cuffs and tobacco smell went on his way. Rufkin hopped out of his wicker basket and ran out to the woods to play with the trolls.

The Collector congratulated himself, sloping out of the village and still scribbling as he went. A good one. Still, there was one thing that nagged. The slipper had been made of glass, she had said, if he understood the dialect. Most impractical. And most unfolkloric, there wasn't a square inch of glass in the village. That wouldn't do, wouldn't do at all. The gentleman wouldn't like it. Maybe she had meant fur. That made more sense. The two words were similar in sound. And fur might be the same word as leather in this valley talk. He glanced round at the dismal brick tepees. It wasn't like they needed a lot of words for things.

Still, she had told it well. He could picture it, the stiff cold glass slipper slipping perfectly round the pale toes.

He had let his mind wander inadvisably, for as he rounded the corner he found himself facing a portly figure with a feather in his green felt hat and a splintery axe handle resting lightly over one shoulder. Two bearded lads with chests like oxen were there to back him up.

"Grüß Gott" said the mayor.

"Most costly it proved."

Jakob Grimm scowled. He had had years of this money grubbing twit. It was lunchtime, May was in the air and the asparagus was ripening in the fields, but still here he was listening to the man complain.

"Get me some wine, Wilhelm" he snapped at his bovine brother who was hovering, having answered the door. Wilhelm trudged obediently off.

"It proved a most costly trip." The Collector was still saying. "a most costly....expedition. These peasants only understand money, they have no feeling for the finer things in life, like ..." he was obviously going to say "like us", but thought it might seem presumptuous. "...like yourself."

Jakob leafed through the grubby notes, tsk-ing at the misspellings.

Hold on, he thought. Something was wrong.

"Sir," he said, looking up over his spectacles, "I don't understand how the shoe thing works. It is a nice conceit but surely fur shoes are not so individual that they would only fit one foot. Maybe a well worn country boot, but these fur slippers. They would be all floppy."

The man couldn't think of anything to say for quite a while.

"The word might have been leather." he offered at length.

Jakob dropped his eyes to the notes again.

Leather. Leather shoes. Brilliant. Very poetic. Like those ghastly Swedish tales with their iron spears, wooden ships, as though there was any other sort.

"Some peasants have wooden shoes."

Not from their fairy godmother.

"Anyway, surely they should be made of something more valuable, more princely, like gold. That would work. Are you sure she did not say gold?"

The man looked relieved.

"Now you mention it, sir, I believe she may have."

Jakob looked hard at him. Sometimes he wondered if he was making it all up.

Later, down in the cluttered cellar of his print shop, Wilhelm Grimm was weary but at peace, working methodically at what he loved best. The sun had long gone down unnoticed and his Maß of beer had been drawn and had stood untouched for an hour, a treat for the bulky old compositor, a reason to finally stop the endless fiddling and declare the typesetting done. Three times he had coughed, wiped his huge inky hands on his moustache and sat down to take the froth off the beer. Twice he had paused before it touched his mouth, and got up again to reset some kerning or tweak the leads. Time had worn on, it was nearly midnight and he was finally happy, almost. As the flat beer neared his lips for the third time he felt something trouble him, not quite a thought, more like the memory of a dream or a pattern in the smoke. With it came the absolute certainty that he had missed something.

He stalked back to stare at the wooden print frame with its 16 pages of lead type. All correct. He turned to the desk and squinted laboriously at his brother's manuscript, scored with angry edits. Then turned back to the frame again. There.

"tooF reh morf llef reppilS dlog a delf ehs sa"

That line was perfectly spaced but just too short, half a millimetre. He considered adding a comma. Ugly. Could he add a letter? Most of the line was workaday stuff but there was one adjective. He stared again.

The "reppilS dlog".

That was right. He checked against the manuscript once more. "gold slipper". "reppilS dlog". Yes. No, it just didn't look right.

Suddenly, he knocked out the form of print, picked up a font tray in his meaty hands and started slotting deftly away at the frame.

"tooF reh morf llef reppilS ssalg a delf ehs sa" he wrote.

Then he sat down for the last time and after a moment's satisfied reflection took a long slow pull on his Maß.

Behind him, propped unheeded against the wall, the printer's mirror showed the frame and there in the middle minutely reflected the new line:

"as she ran a glass Slipper fell from her Foot."

Back in the valley, when the Collector had left and the boy scarpered, the old woman sat for a while picking at her gone-out pipe. Then, she wandered meditatively over to the corner and jiggled a loose brick. Behind the wall was a linen bundle, which unwrapped to reveal a silken shawl and safe within a thing. An old thing, that caught the firelight with a rippling sheen.

She had liked it. She had just liked it the first time she felt it.

She put it carefully in its place on the mantelpiece.

She stoked up the fire, sat down, relit the half-pipeful and gazed at the translucent patterns, letting her mind drift back to another light, the light of the warm south, seeing herself, as if from outside, kneeling on the marble flags, with her honest eyes and metal bucket of dirty water, as – "Bastardo, Bastardo," – the Cardinal's ugly old mistress came flying down, rippling and naked with her clothes spilling from her arms, and passed her with a splash.

And the Cardinal behind shouting "Bella, Bella!"

She was young and stared shamelessly.

"Bella, Bella!"

The Cardinal swept by.

"Bella, Bella."

Without taking her eyes off him she slipped her hand into the bucket.

She could feel it there, where it had fallen. The thing.

She smiled and blew out a big dirty ball of blue grey smoke.

# Geep

Jeannie always loved filling in forms but this one was special, this one was for her baby. She leaned back into the springy plastic orange chair in the waiting room and stopped herself from sucking the pen.

Gender? it asked.

Easy. Female.

They meant hers not the baby's. Bit stupid in the ante-natal clinic. Still, she filled it in dutifully.

Days to term (approx.). Trickier.

She dug out her mobile. She had an app that counted down showing a stork carrying a baby for each day left. All you had to do was input the start date and she was pretty sure she had that right.

It had all begun during a late-working bank holiday at the petting zoo. Their first llama was about to be born. Llamas were a long-standing feature, popular with the children for their soft wool, but their pack had never bred, though they did gather together in a corner of their paddock to defecate socially. Evening was wearing on and she should have been home, but kept coming back to see the doe lying there with its wide eyes, scared and animal. She supposed there was something else going on in its simple soul too, something wholly absorbing that outweighed the fear and the pain.

Samson, the doe's mate, was grazing away in a far corner of the field. She looked at him long and hard. You don't get much back from a llama, she had discovered, and thought of Michael back at home, rooting around in the fridge without managing to cook anything. She looked hard at Samson again.

The llama was, in a way, her baby. She had been the one who had found the sponsorship, applying again and again to funders across the English-speaking world. She had registered with the Lima zoo for sperm, wading through mounds of badly translated documentation.

It took forever but eventually, shortly after she had moved in with Michael, the precious packet had arrived in its cool-pak. She had watched with anxious pride as the vet loaded up his turkey baster and approached the nervous animal. Twelve months on this was her triumph, too. She was the quiet sort, though, and didn't want to boast. She just carried on, encouraged by this early success, with her applications.

Funding continued to trickle in and there were long discussions among the beardy board members about which animals should be helped, which were endangered, even if only mildly, and which were good box office. It was the nanny goat that did it. It was a scrawny solitary beast and never got a mention at the meetings. She would pass its paddock every day and, looking into its weird striped eyes, felt that it was the ugliest thing she had ever seen. She began filling in forms.

A week later she got rotated to muck out the meerkats by the entrance. The post-van pulled up.

"Hi there, Jeannie." sang out the postman, whose name she always forgot.

"Hi there," she answered, "anything special?"

"Package to sign for," he said presenting a digital screen and a plastic pen. She filled in the sections, sucking the pen occasionally between boxes, and signed with a well-practised signature. Then she wiped the pen. "Sorry," she said, hiding her nerves behind a flirty smile.

"Turkey?" said Michael, "Again."

"I thought you liked turkey?"

"I do. Lucky me." he said placidly. "It's like Christmas every week." She looked at him for a long time as he bent in and chewed. Chew, chew, chew.

The goat was a sensation. First when the vet pronounced it pregnant no-one could work out how it had happened. There were local farms of course but while sheep were common goats were rare, mainly kept as pets, and none of the farmers remembered any escaping for a night on the tiles. The likely explanation only became clear when scans revealed something wrong and the nanny goat gave birth to a litter of two male goats, one still-born female and...a geep – a cross-breed between goat and sheep. Someone had blundered. The zoo hired a PR man and the staff began shaving regularly and posing with the geep for the local - then national - then international press. Jeannie could sometimes be seen at the back of these pictures, or just on the edge of the shot. The nanny-goat seemed to derive no pleasure from her motherhood or her celebrity and mooched on much as before.

"You're late," remarked Michael, "again." as Match of the Day wound down toward the weekend's goalless draws.

"Yes, this new place is killing me. I like working with the animals but it's all the admin." Jeannie had moved on to a new job, at an animal breeding centre for the pet industry. She was a star at dealing with the intricate and complex formalities and recently the guinea pigs had been giving cause for concern.

The first guinea pig with a tail was considered a mutation. However, it was kept alive and was able to produce a new brood. After that it just kept getting stranger. The new strain began to defecate together in one corner. This was potentially an asset, as anyone who has kept guinea pigs will know, and some of the later generations had the most gorgeous soft fur. This was a winner. Management at the breeding centre began seriously considering their marketing strategy, except that the damn things would keep spitting.

"Applying for another job?" queried Michael from his sofa. Jeannie was wholly absorbed, her face washed by the blue light of the laptop. As a man who liked a comfortable life Michael found all this moving onward and upward troubling. Still the money would be useful, they were planning a baby. Hopefully she would be smart enough not to mention that at interview.

Jeannie's fingers danced over the keys. She loved filling in forms at the best of times but this one was special, this one was for her baby.

# Alanna McIntyre

*I am a regular
attendee of NightWriters.
I wrote "Rethreading My Life" which
is about loss. Coming to terms
with bereavement I have
rediscovered that gardening,
felting, pottery, yoga, meditation,
writing and acting make me
happy. I also help look after my
grandchildren Kaia and Umi which
gives me joy.*

# February

Light filters into eyes,
Hurriedly dress, grab camera and keys
Walk up the hill, cross the road
To the Downs where warm yellow swirls
Amidst ruddy hues marble the horizon
Changing from moment to moment.
Now clouds blush pink
Outstretched wings, black silhouettes,
Swoop the sky part patched with blue
Warm tones converge and melt in the mist
Now settle to a grey blue day.
Feel cold and speed home
Luxuriate in central heating
And the momentary awe
Of a new born February morning.

# Stories Need Tellers

The preparation of the grate
With paper, kindling and log
Gives the story its place and arc.
The striking of the match
Lights the paper
Sparks the watcher's imagination
Flames flicker, ideas flutter
Grey doubt twirls in acrid smoke
Disperses as flames take hold
Free to dance with delight
In blue edged, red orange flamenco dresses.
Characters appear spiralling upwards
From different places whose voices
Cackle and hiss as they devour wood.
Mesmerised eyes see performing trapeze artistes
Shape shifters, unleashed.
In their fascination food for fire is forgotten
Emblazoned pictures on the retina
Fade to red embers in the ash
A reminder that this tale has come to an end.

Alanna McIntyre

# A Meditative Experience

Time slows as the ship approaches the lock
 A meditative experience
The light turns green, the lock gates open and the ship glides in
Fenders lowered, act as buffers.
Ropes are attached to keep the ship steady.
The lock gates close and the water swooshes in
The ship is in dark dankness.
Eyes measure the ship's upward progress
By the ladder rungs fixed at the side of the lock.
Over the next thirty five minutes
The ship inches herself back into the light and landscape.
The required water level is reached.
Pause, wait for the red signal to turn to green.
Ties are unfastened, fenders raised
Lock gates open and the heron who stood sentinel
Flies off and the ship slips free to cruise on.

# The Bowl

The bowl's cupped shape is ready to receive and give
Formed in clay where thumb and finger work together
Rhythmically stroking from the base upwards,
Thumb inside, index mirrors the pressure from outside.
The other hand turns, supports as sides are smoothed
And thinned, organically shape evolves.
The mind meditates feeling for evenness
In the burnt sienna coloured clay.
The clay now no longer pliable
Hands leave the bowl to rest and harden.
Fired in the kiln the dark reddish brown hue
Transforms to charcoal black.
When pinged the bowl
Resonates with a healing sound
Accept and receive, receive and give.

Alanna McIntyre

# The Sky's Washing

Have you noticed the sky's washing?
Sometimes there's the skimpiest negligee hanging
Opaque in the blue. Other times neat lines of sheets
Billowing in the wind. Grey black stained
Shapes threaten, hang glowering with
Thoughts of rain, ashamed of their grey gloom.
They want to sparkle white.
Sloppy ill scratched lines
Pegged by reluctant droopy drawered teenagers
Forced from cowering under sheets.
Candy flossed swirls curl
Teasing the blue into thinking
They are delectable.
Sometimes the sky is blue rinsed.
Early morning can reveal baby pink
Suits flying in the sky. At dusk suddenly a myriad of colours
Fire in line vying to be seen
Leaving an afterglow shown in
Strangers smiling and lovers holding hands.

# The Pavement Is Paper

The pavement is paper.
Pastels are the colours. You smear
Their shades lovingly into the paving stone,
State you are homeless and name your dog
On a piece of recycled card.
You accept gifts of food,
Soft drinks, change and notes with gratitude.
Your hat collects coins from passers-by.
Each donation receives a thank you
But your eye and hand concentrate
On the patterned tones you are tinting
Red turns pinkish as you add white
A hint of yellow for warmth.
The way you paint the pavement with reverie
Stays with me for the rest of the day.

# Jam Sandwich

Bread and butter routine
Life slapped into place
Automatic pilot on
Work iron wash feed
Perfunctory clean
Phrases float to mind
Gelled on paper to
Fruit later on, in a
Jam sandwich.

Alanna McIntyre

# Rage

Sitting in tentacled silence
Entrenched in rage.
Ripped free in a primal scream
Sharp colours splay like
Catherine wheels.

# There Are No Words

You ask for words
But there are no words
They would banish the moment
It is –
– just  that –
Definition would
Draw finite lines.
You cannot hear
Your question needs no answer
Words will shatter
Inept – impotent –
Screechy chalk on board
Your question –
My sound internalised goes
Unnoticed.

# Alex Lovell

*At the time of writing, I am a 29 year old writer who lives in Brighton. I want to discuss the important things about what I see and feel every day, both big and small, in a meaningful way and to spark that discussion using imaginative writing. In other words, please enjoy the writing! I blog at https://digitaltreelovell.wordpress.com, play gigs which you can find at http://www.trimtabjim.com and http://failedpsychics.bandcamp.com/release*

*So yeah, drop by if you're interested.*

# Custard

"...had turned to custard."

The reader flipped the paper to the back of the documents, and tapped them into order on the surface of the desk like a newsreader. A collective "mmm" filled the top floor of the pub room, like everyone had tasted something delicious at the same time.

One friendly younger member of the group wondered whether to speak first, but stopped. The reader thought that the "mmm" hadn't been quite as definitive as he'd liked. Sure enough, as he glanced from side to side, taking in the expressions, nobody seemed to have the confidence or an overwhelming desire to speak, and the unearthly black silence weighed for quite an uncomfortable length of time. It sent a shiver down his spine.

He smirked hopefully towards no-one in particular as he waited for the first reaction. He wondered if it was the calm before the storm or just empty silence. He already feared the reactions would probably be more out of pity than help.

Most were smiling with eyes shut and fingers to lips in a monk-like pose. He grasped onto the side of the desk and moved his chair forwards.

"Well, yes, very...very interesting..." came the first reply, from the leader of the group, "well I thought that it was generally very interesting... you really got into... got into the head of someone who's been put... or rather that puts themselves under that kind of pressure to receive what he justifies as merited validation from others."

The leader leaned over the desk and pushed back his reading glasses to read from his notes.

"Just some tiny little nitpicks though," he said, "you seem to use some superfluous words. For example, I thought when you said '*quite*' twice during one section. And when you say 'reading glasses' you can probably just say glasses. After that you have 'read' which is fine - if you have read you don't need to say glasses."

The reader scribbled on the paper in red pen and muttered "thank you."

He gave a sharp intake of breath and looked hopefully towards the other members. One person, sitting Buddha-like at the edge of the table, was wondering when he would have the chance to speak, he leaned forward.

"How about the characters?" said the reader, "did they feel real?"

"Well, they were not properly defined," said someone, "I thought that the narrator took precedence and we didn't get enough information about the others."

One of the older, more experienced critics inhaled sharply and leant forwards.

"If I may be so bold," he said, "it is riddled with mistakes. You are repeating adjectives all over the place. And there are many places within the text where you suffer from a novice writer's disease, often known as 'adjectival obesity," where you believe that the important shades of meaning within the text must be filled in with meticulously precise adjectives. For example, at some point, you mention something like a huge deafening calm or something like that... you can just say 'a calm.' That's fine in and of itself, the listener will fill in their own information within their own minds..."

There was another gap before anyone could react. The characteristics of the people around the room seemed to be very scattered - they were either fit as fiddles or old as the hills. He gave a huge deathly sigh and leaned back.

"You use too many clichés," said someone, "and your writing is full of shifts in perspective. At one point I think you shift to one person at the start of the paragraph and then back to the author in the next sentence, which is still in the same paragraph. You can't just shift perspectives like that... it confuses the reader."

"Well I rather liked it," interjected one of the female listeners, "I liked the ambiguity. It had a lot of potential. What I felt was that the narrator likes to imagine all of these different perspectives belonging to different people, feeding the author's sense of unease under self-inflicted pressure, and that came across well."

"Yes but it wasn't clear," came the reply, "to me that's a classic 101 of bad writing."

"I liked it," said one of the others, one of the spring beans, "but you need to keep your punctuation under control."

"It's very interesting though, I liked the punctuation, it gave it a loose feel -"

"Me too."

"It's just too all over the place though. You never know who's speaking. And I'm pretty sure you repeat some of the descriptions."

The author sat back and sighed. He wrote a few notes on his paper in red ink.

"No, it's good," said one more of the regulars, a person whose stuttering and cerulean eyes locked onto him. "It was very rough. There were all those mistakes above. But I thought the style was strong enough to carry it," she blinked, "it was rough, but throughout I was enthralled by this person. You know, the whole story was about one person's quest for validation and it really rubbed off on me. I liked it."

The author smiled at her understanding and corona-like smile.

"Thank you," he replied to her.

"Yes well," said one of the regulars, "I do think the idea and the story were good. It's just too bad that everything around it had turned to custard."

# Fish

Nicola shook this morning's package - Tidal Power Textbooks N-Z - up by her ear and smiled. It sounded like it contained lots of lessons, and she had always liked tidal power. She tore it open and chose a USB.

She turned on the switch by the window. Her eyes followed the trickling sound across the wall, and then she closed them to listen to the soothing hum of machines fading in around her.

The glass door in the corner flung open. Familiar blue patterns lit up on the console behind it.

"Good morning Nicola," said the door.

"Good morning," she said, "did you sleep well?"

"Yes. I observed that you had a very troubling dream last night," it opened a small drive containing a glass of water and a green pill, "this will help."

"Yeah, it was scary," she swallowed the pill, "I was flying through a black void filled with distant silver dots, and riding an air bicycle."

"Yes. Sounds... scary. Please step into the booth and insert a lesson."

"Do you really think... I'll be an important Palace engineer?"

"I think so. Well, only fourteen days until you find out!"

"OK."

Nicola had just taken her first step into the booth when an emerging dance of colours turned her head. A white, orange and black shape was darting around behind the glass window, moving entirely at whim, its body shimmering gloriously in the light.

Nicola stepped out from the booth, hands clasped over her open mouth, pupils following every move.

"Please commence your lesson now, Nicola," intoned the door.

She followed the thing with her finger and giggled.

"Wow!" she cried, "it... it's a fish!"

"Fish are extinct, Nicola. Gone like the ice caps. Step back into the booth please."

She jumped around, laughing, and skipped across the floor, chanting her words with delight, then sat watching the fish at the window, leaning left as the fish flicked right.

"NICOLA!"

She flicked the switch. The voice died. The hum faded. She sat watching the fish by the glow of the sea until it was gone, then wiped away a tear.

# Steady Hands

Q1.

Yeah, hello...yeah, it's going. It's going...it's going alright. [laughs] alright. Can you see my number? That's my landline.

Q2.

Yeah, nice to meet you and all that Jason, but for now, first and foremost, I gotta ask you a... two favours now alright? Sorry if they sounds rude. [laughs]

Q3.

Yeah, uh...it's pretty simple actually. A bit arrogant, really, but then again I've given up on... on being nice, you know? I need a real shake-up. Every day I wake up and hundreds of truths and realities are confronting me the way I am and exposing me to be vacuous and hollow, but they don't... they don't change anything, you know? And all these truths just cause the water to rise higher below my neck, and then I use something - alcohol, internet, cigarettes, to calm it down. But the water's still rising, you know? [laughs] still rising and still about to drown me and all I can do is hold my breath...

Q4.

Oh sorry, the favour was simple. Sorry I'm gonna get like that, I didn't even tell you the important part before I started ranting. It's simple man, whenever I say question, that's the only time you can ask a question, right. Otherwise it's just me and my rants. And the second one is, you must not tell anyone my address or where I live. Question?

Q5.

Oh, don't give me a name, man. My parents gave me one and all... and all it did was just become an adhesive for all their irrational despondency. That's what therapists do, isn't it? They give their fucking anger a name and it becomes more like a person, a reality. My parents did that with me. Question.

Q6.

Just call me mate, OK? You're my mate. [laughs] I trust you. Question.

Q7.

Well, some fags, a sofa, a little razor on the cushion next to it, the sea hurtling out there against the black malleable void, some seagulls...that's it really. Question.

Q8.

Yeah, it was just there. Question.

Q9.

Well, I'm thinking about the great empty, thinking about death, so the razors are for the cutting and the cigarettes are to make sure my hand is fucking steady enough that I don't fuck it up. I can't...can't concentrate without them...can't...I can't fuck it up- I don't want to be a failure in suicide like in life, you know? [laughs] Question.

Q10.

Well...I haven't been a failure in life. I've just been bafflingly unnecessary in life. Question.

Q11.

Well I had an altercation. You know...a verbal Mexican stand-in. Question.

Q12.

Stand-off, sorry. Yeah, you didn't correct that. I just did cause I'm a dick. But maybe not as big a dick as this dick in the Co-op just now. Some security guard who was far too involved in his job and seems to think he's special and saw me reading a magazine. I was sitting, reading a music magazine. It was some piece of shit. I need to know about music, you know. I need... I need some guidance to know why I should like what I guess I like, so I can exhaust that one and find another stimulus, and this search for stimulus gives me a reason... uh... well and this walking bag of manure comes up and past me right, and says: do you plan to read that or just buy it? The fucking nerve! I was reading it for like two minutes and he comes and regurgitates his vested one-for-all power over my happiness. Then he turns round and tells his mate. And surprisingly, more than anything else that's fucked up with my life - and there's a lot- that's the thing made me want to kill myself. Question.

Q13.

Yeah, well, I know I did something wrong, and he knew that I did something wrong, but the idea that he can only do his work by abusing people... abuse. Instead of being nice and direct and actually tell people what we want in all honesty, we throw a nuke at an archery target. And that nuke is sarcasm. Of course I was wrong. But it's convinced me no-one can communicate genuinely anymore. Question.

Q14.

My job? It's OK. I do stuff. It's creative. I don't know. Ask me a better question. Question.

Q15.

Oh, no, I don't have a romantic relationship, and I doubt I ever will again. That's a good point. I used to... I used to have a good relationship with women... but... let's not look at that, you know? Question.

Q16.

I don't want to talk about that. Question.

Q17.

Well, the best questions also have a ton of platitudes and retorts and Wildean shit that I've memorised but now means nothing to me. It's all numbing and useless. Well... it didn't used to be, you know? [laughs]. I read Holden Caulfield... what's that one? Catcher in The Rye? And Bukowski? And they seemed real. Sentences just hit home and reflected inside me like they were my own. Like sledgehammers. Now when I read or listen or do stuff like that it never works. It's like my own mind has forgotten how to empathise. That's it! Holy shit man. I can't empathise. That's what it is. Nothing hits home like it used to, and I need that rush. I try and reproduce it in my own work but then no-one will read that crap. Well, apart from Alison, but forget that. Question.

Q18.

Alison? Uh...forget I said that. It's unimportant. Question.

Q19.

Nah, forget about that. If I start talking about her then you'll start talking about how I have a bond with a caring female spirit and how that'll be my saving grace. Truth is I did have some sort of relationship with a female. But then again everybody does. It just got to the point where after two years the idea of being together is no worse than being single. [sniffing]. Being single comes with independence but solitude of buzzing, relentless thoughts. And being together is... not as good. I can't be poetic but it's not good. Question.

Q20.

Yeah. [sound of cigarette being lit] I needed that. Question.

Q21.

No worse than being on a phone for 50 hours a week like some twat I know. Question.

Q22.

No, never diagnosed. But I am depressed. I'm thinking of taking my own life, huh, I guess that must count for something. But I don't think anyone who witnesses the world as it is can possibly not be depressed, you know, and calling it depression to feel angry about the state of the world and, uh, you know, to call it a disease, is like saying... is like saying that you find water... you find... I don't know, like say... you find a cat...is like calling a man mad 'cause he finds water wet, you know? Overpopulation, lack of truth, um, broken families. The world is depressing. Sorry that's such a cliché. I'm sure you hear that from fucking everyone. But yeah. Question.

Q23.

Yeah there are a lot of good things in the world yeah, but more worse things. Question.

Q24.

Really? Have you made a comparison chart? Question.

Q25.

What family? Question.

Q26.

A few friends, but no-one who'll miss me. Question.

Q27.

I don't have a job, no. But I do think that the world would be better without another paranoid, directionless neurotic with a bunch of failed half-digested artistic sentiments lying in his chewed-up bedroom? Because I think so. Question.

Q28.

Are you saying you're not sick of listening to me? Question.

Q29.

Well, you could be going bowling, I don't know, writing, singing, uh, I don't know, dressing up as a seagull and scaring old ladies... Question.

Q30.

No, I'm not fooling anyone. But if my parents, family and friends won't miss me and I want to rid myself of this world, why not? Question.

Q31.

No-one will miss me. You sure as hell won't.

Q32.

Don't talk out of turn. I'm sorry though…

Q33.

Well...you broke the rule. And you did it again now. You spoke out of turn.

Q34.

Nah mate, that's it. You've been a good friend - a very good friend - but that's it really. It's finished. You did a good job mate, I'll call you back if I decide on anything. I'd better be talking to you when I call back. Question.

Q35.

Yes. Bye. [phone cuts off]

Q1.

Yes, [name].

Q2.

I work for [company name].

Q3.

Yes, well...yes I did...I talked to him on the night in question.

Q4.

Well yes, I'm obviously very sorry about his current condition.

Q5.

Do I really? Do you want exact timings or...

Q6.

OK, well about [time deleted], I received a phone call from him, a typical one like we do at [company name], and did what we are trained to do, which is to immediately establish a rapport with the suicidal person. Different suicidal people have different needs. Some require consolation, some require problem-solving and some just require an ear. The man in question was one of those.

Q7.

Well yes, he talked. Very typical suicidal thoughts - dependency, powerlessness, psychobabble... he seemed to require a conduit, I think, to his thoughts, so he would work them out. They do a typical depressed thing of trying to dig a hole into their depressed thoughts so deeply that they can find something unique, um, something they hadn't witnessed before... to snap them out of it.

Q8.

Yes, I broke his first rule, and he hung up on me.

Q9.

Well, yeah, then I broke his second, I know. I had to do my job. I don't care if I broke his trust. You have to try everything to save someone's life, even if they don't realise they want it.

Q10.

I'm not sure.

Q11.

Well, I'd like to think so. [laughs] That's my job, to delay the impulse enough. Can I see the life I saved?

Q12.

OK, I'll wish him all the best. Thank you officer.

# B

*I am a long time member of Brighton NightWriters, attending from 2006 when writing my fictional poker novel 'Under The Gun: Poker Highs and Lows'. Since then moving into the field of video editing also, I have a website showcasing both my short stories and miscellaneous video projects, webspace23.com.*

# The Self Bettering Class

Yeah yeah, thought Richards while Abel (UnAbel he should have been called) carried on with his uninspiring spiel. Who the hell could take seriously an ageing hippy vegan who dismissed rotting fermenting dead animals in the gum in his rolling papers as being an urban myth? Who even when presented with the facts of the matter in an undoctored print out from Google, could just keep on toking this up contentedly. This hypocrite was an ugly ageing hippy vegan at that - one who, just looking at for more than two seconds straight, you wanted to punch into better shape. And here he was as good as announcing himself leader of the spiritual evolution. Stupid cunt.

Richards had the same feelings when looking at himself in the mirror, but he didn't generally admit that to anyone, least of all himself, instead he just avoided doing so. He had grown a thick beard. He hated beards, but hated looking at himself more. In mentally referring to others as ageing he chose not to think about his own fast slipping away years in this incarnation. That was thirty nine, though he had stopped counting at twenty three. At thirty nine he found himself single, jobless, with no children or purpose, but not sure if either of those latter two were the goal. Not being sure what the goal was had always done his head in. He'd looked for answers in casual (protected) sex, mind altering drugs and religion (at times in combination), but all had been dead ends. The religion particularly he had given the boot. This Abel cunt - who by some amazing fluke did have a missus and a kid - was now claiming that he, of all motherfuckers, had the answers.

As he babbled on these no doubt LSD or magic mushrooms induced answers, the bit of beard he had (just a clump below his left cheek) jittered. No one knew for sure if this was a deliberate attempt to be individual, or create a new facial hair fashion statement, or whether he just started shaving each day from the same area of face, and each day (each day being stoned out of his mind before even making his morning coffee) forgot what he was doing and stopped shaving at the same point. Yet the others still all seemed to be actually listening to what this forty year old fruitcake was saying.

"We are all One," were the words coming out of his mouth as this tenth of a beard broke out into a jig, "but aspects of this One are currently not working for Us. We need to put work in on the dark elements within Us, being mindful of our own thoughts and actions, and that in turn will help take care of those on the external."

Richards waited for an explanation of how exactly that would take care of those on the external, but one wasn't forthcoming. Instead the jigging slowed down and after a brief pause - perhaps for applause, which Richards was pleased to see wasn't forthcoming either - Abel launched into a guided group meditation: "Now, if you would kindly each find yourselves a comfortable meditation posture, let's clear Our mind and witness the truth within..."

Richards waited for someone to start pissing themselves with laughter, or at least a stifled giggle, but instead they all silently shuffled into half lotus positions on the grubby squat floor or straightened their backs if lucky enough to have got a chair, and with nicotine stained hands folded in front of them, closed their eyes, taking this shit seriously, the muppets. He looked back over at Abel, who was looking at him, and now nodded at him for him to do the same. You total nitwit, thought Richards at him, but he obliged and creaked his legs together, dropping his own yellowed hands on top of these. He waited for Abel to close his eyes first (a few seconds of staring each other out before he did) and then he shut his.

"OK, so let us let dhama do its work," Abel's stupid voice rambled through the darkness, "irregardless of what you may think of me..."

Regardless, not irregardless, you numpty, thought Richards, then considering the next bit, wondered if that had been aimed directly towards him.

"... let us give a fair trial to this technique - not mine, but as passed down by The Buddha."

How generous of you to give Sid a bit of credit Richards, through his closed eyes, sneered.

Gonggg, the sound of a metal disc being struck with a mallet, vibrated.

And boom, he was this supposed 'man who woke up' Siddhārtha Gautama having his eureka moment - like Isaac Newton, sat beneath a tree. Enlightenment? or some other such illusion of grandeur. How splendid. Was he fuck. He was still unenlightened (but happy to at least know that). Richards asked himself 'What in the name of frig are you even doing here on a Saturday night when you could be down the pub, getting ready for a party or doing just about anything else?'

Abel's voice droned on, "Empty your mind. Fix your attention on the breath entering and exiting through your nose."

Richards caught his attention fixing on a mental image of getting hold of and tugging Abel's bit of beard until the skin tore to reveal a Terminator style skeleton, but he played ball and diverted it from there to try to follow this instruction. OK, breath in, breath out, a piece of piss, you can do this.

"Ignore everything else,"

I'm trying to ignore you, you fucker..., thought Richards.

"... and just observe."

Richards observed his attention had gone again. He watched his monkey mind swing from thought branch - 'I could murder a spliff' - to thought branch - 'I could murder this Abel twat' - to thought branch - 'Why can't I keep my attention on my breath for more than a fraction of a second?'

Craving, aversion, frustration.

"Be gentle with yourself," continued Abel, "if you find your mind wandering, just gently bring it back to the breath..."

The reason he was here was that, in spite of not having found the answers in all his other searching, he was still cursed with being a seeker, albeit a highly disillusioned and cynical one by this late age. Just give it a go, he told himself. Then, when it doesn't work, you can rip the piss out of this idiot for being another fraudster fake. The breath, man, focus on the breath.

At least ten minutes had passed and Richards had focused on his breath for a maximum duration of two seconds, the rest of this time watching eyelid movies of pornography, drug taking and mindless violence. Well, first imagining them on his eyelids, then finding himself in these scenes. Whenever Abel spoke, he would drag himself back out of these, and once again be sat there with himself, whereupon he would fast grow uncomfortable and again try to focus on his breath, be distracted again, and go back into another daydream. Thoughts that would occasionally occur between all this were along the lines of that initial 'Why can't I keep my attention on my breath for more than a fraction of a second? things like 'What the fuck' and 'How come I have no control whatsoever of my own mind?'

In the alone with himself time he saw the things he hid from others - all of his many life regrets - to which trying to focus on the breath, or inevitably ending up daydreaming, were both preferable. Regrets like his lying, stealing, causing harm to others, especially harm to others who had been foolish enough to care about him even when knowing about the first three. The pain in his legs and in his back were nothing on the pain he felt there.

"You may feel some physical discomfort," Abel was saying, "but don't react to this - just observe the fact and return your attention to the breath. Likewise, if you happen to be feeling any pleasant sensations, don't react to those with any attachment."

Richards was finding himself attached to one of the bloodier violent daydreams he had found himself in, but like the head of Abel that he had stomped a Doc Marten boot down on in that daydream, this popped and there he was again, cross-legged on a squat floor surrounded by hippies sitting in their own worlds and thoughts. He hoped lost in their own worlds and thoughts rather than studiously observing their breath all this time and he the only one unable to.

Another ten minutes passed, or it felt like it could have been more than that, maybe twenty, or thirty, or not out of question a full hour, Richards was wondering how much longer this would go on for. His legs and back were throbbing like crazy now, but through the small slits of partly open eyelids he saw that no other fucker had moved. God be damned if he was going to before one of these did. Abel was still speaking, but leaving longer gaps of far stretching silence between each string of words: "The breath going in, the breath going out..." Silence... Silence... Silence...

Richards wanted the others to be going through the same levels of pain that he was, but at the same time felt an odd kind of sympathy for them if they were. Not as strong as the sympathy he felt for himself of course, but nonetheless it was there.

"May all beings be happy, peaceful and liberated," Abel was now saying.

And relax.

Wheee.

The meditators opened eyes, unclasped hands, uncrossed legs.

This in itself is a liberation. Richards had to admit to himself that he did feel better for that.

"So," said Abel, "through this you all will have probably noticed the extent of the wild mind, how difficult it is to train, and also had a taster of our true nature of impermanence."

Richards noticed that his feelings of violence towards Abel on seeing his face again had decreased. While he still felt an inkling to punch him, he no longer had the desire to keep on pummelling him into oblivion. Maybe it was the bliss of being out of that meditation experience, and that Abel's "May all beings be happy, peaceful and liberated," had been what had ended it. Whatever it was, he appreciated this moment's almost peace.

After the talk and meditation, as the other let's-try-meditationers spilled out of the squat and onto the street, Richards went so far as to thank Abel for this (or the meditation part of it anyway): "Found it kind of interesting."

"I'm glad to hear it," Abel beamed at him, and gave him a namaste bow, "I benefited from learning this in India you know, so felt compelled to share it."

"You know there's a bit on your face you missed shaving?" Richards asked him.

"I know," he said.

"You still use those animal gum rolling papers?" Richards continued with the questions.

"Actually, no," said Abel, "I switched to another confirmed vegan brand after you informed me of that, for which I am grateful to you for letting me know."

"No probs," said Richards, and decided to leave his intended further interrogation at that. For now. Having had to face so many of his own fuck ups through that short period of sitting trying to focus on his breath, who was he to judge another anyway.

Regrets, he'd had a few. Thinking of having a few, his monkey mind leapt to pub, which he suggested to Abel, who said, "Sure, that sounds good. Shall I roll one for the road first?"

# Freddie Harnett

*This is my first attempt at writing a play. It's kind of an amalgamation of my life experiences with a humorous twist.*

# Grange Hill for Grown Ups

### Act 1 Scene 1:

*Audience enters to the theme tune of 'Grange Hill'. Theme tune fades out and black out.*

**Pink Floyd:** *(Brick in the wall)* 'We don't need no education. We don't need no false control. No sarcasm in the classroom. Teacher. Leave them kids alone'.

*Lights up on teacher preparing for lesson on board. Classroom is dreary – as colourless as possible. We can hear gale force winds outside. It is clear that this is an RE classroom from the pictures on the wall – a picture of Buddha, Virgin Mary and Adam and Eve. Eve has been graffitied over. Her breasts have been crossed out, and a large penis has been drawn over her fig leaf. There is one boy and one girl (Studious girl and Gaylord) sitting apart copying what the teacher is writing on the board. They are clearly cold, sitting in their jackets, blowing on their hands trying to keep warm. A group of girls enter including gang leader Tanisha. They open the door, and enter. They are struggling to shut the door against the wind. As the gang walks into lesson they are hanging onto Tanisha's every word. It is immediately apparent that she is 'top dog'.*

**Tanisha:** So, anyways yeah, Tashika said that Tamika said that Tevena said that Tilisha said that Toshina said that Tylissa said that Tyrone said that Tamwar said that Toshi said that Tonilililooloo saw yous two kissing outside the Premier Inn. Is dat true, yeah?

**Taqueria:** We did more than kiss yeah. I got the photos to prove it.

**Tanisha:** Oh my days, I swear down I thought dese fings was illegal man.

**Sir:** Phone away please Taqueria. Tanisha, what have you done to yourself?

**Tanisha:** It's my new afro innit. You like?

**Sir:** I'm sorry love. You're gonna have to brush that out. It's against school policy.

**Tanisha:** I don't think so!! It is the epitome of the stereotypical teenager to express their inherent life state, their moods, their swagger, their inner demons, artistic freedom and creativity through their physical appearance, innit!

**Sir:** There's no point talking to her.

**Tanisha:** You can take my freedom, you can take my school uniform, but you will never take my afro!

**Sir:** Come on; now, write what's on the board. And, get rid of your gum Tanisha. Everyone take your coats off please. (All students groan) You won't feel the benefit of them when go outside.

**Tanisha:** Please sir. It's freezing in here!

**Sir:** I won't say it again. All coats off please!

**Tanisha:** Taqueria you should have boxed that man in the face man. He was well rude!

**Tamara:** Who's that?

**Tanisha:** That bloke in the shop when she was trying to buy her fags.

**Sir:** Concentrate please... Tanisha, I said concentrate.

**Tanisha:** I am concentrating... on applying my make-up. It's an art form Sir. It takes years of dedicated practice, isn't that right, Gaylord.

**Sir:** Taqueria, I said phone away, please. Taqueria, if you don't put your phone away this instant, I'm going to have to take it off you. Right, that's it! Give it here, now!

**Tanisha:** You can't take her phone away Sir. That is violating her human rights, innit. Some would call it stealing.

**Sir:** It's not stealing if you give it back Tanisha.

**Tanisha:** No that's borrowing. But you is taking without permission, which equals stealing.

**Sir:** Can you all please copy the title on the board.

**Tanisha:** I can't write sir. I've got a bad arm.

**Sir:** What exactly is wrong with your arm Tanisha?

**Tanisha:** I broke it Sir.

**Sir:** So, why isn't it in plaster?

**Tanisha:** I've got tennis elbow sir

**Sir:** Do you have a note pertaining to this injury?

**Tanisha:** I've got tendonitis sir.

**Sir:** Have you got a note from home? No, didn't think so. Can you please write down the title?

**Tanisha:** How can I write with my tendonitis, tennis elbow broken arm?

**Sir:** Tanisha, if you refuse to participate in the lesson, I will have no choice but to remove you.

**Tanisha:** I haven't got my glasses, I can't see.

*A couple come skipping into class linking arms. 'Queenie' and 'Bulldog'*

**Bulldog:** Sorry we're late sir. There's a storm brewing outside.

**Sir:** You two are late every single lesson. This is totally unacceptable. Why are you so late?

**Queenie:** Erm, I was having my hair done? *Queenie is bald.*

**Sir:** That doesn't make any sense, does it, Queenie? And like Judge Judy always says 'if it doesn't make sense it's cos....

**All girlgang:** *In unison* It's not true!

**Sir:** You may well hang your head in shame young man. It's not true, is it?.... Cos you're lying aren't you?

**Bulldog:** Allow it man! Let him do his ting! You always need to bother everyone cos you've got no life of your own.

**Sir:** I will not allow it young lady. I have responsibilities, and I take my responsibilities very seriously. Tanisha, I've already told you to get rid of your gum.

**Queenie:** Thanks for standing up for me Bulldog, I love you so much.

**Bulldog:** Oh Queenie. I love me too.

**Tanisha:** I think I'm gonna vomit.

**Sir:** Now, come along class, pay attention please. The title is, 'What has religion done for the world? If this question is too complex for you, you can choose to answer the second question, which is 'What is Prayer?'

**Tanisha:** Sir, you is discriminating. Why don't you just say 'All the suck ups answer question 1, and all the dumb fucks answer question 2.

**Sir:** It's important to differentiate Tanisha, so that you can all achieve.

**Bulldog:** 'What is prayer?'

**Tanisha:** See, dumb fuck!

**Bulldog:** Sir, I know! I know! I know! What is Prayer? Prayer is the courage to persevere. It is the struggle to overcome our own weakness and lack of confidence in ourselves. It is the act of impressing in the very depths of our being the conviction that we can change the situation without fail. Prayer is the way to destroy all fear. It is the way to banish sorrow, the way to light a torch of hope. It is the revolution that rewrites the scenario of our destiny'

**Girl gang:** Shut up/You loser/ when you talk I wanna kill myself/Queenie shut your bitch up/Hush up your gums/Put a muzzle on her/Control your woman!

**Taqueria:** If you don't stop talking I will kill you, chop you up into tiny pieces and feed you to my dog.

**Tanisha:** Your dog's picky though, innit. It has good taste. She probably wouldn't eat her.

**Taqueria:** True dat!

**Queenie:** Why are you such a loser?

**Taylor:** I don't believe in religion Sir

**Sir:** Well, that's great Taylor. And why is that? There must be a reason you're so opposed to religion. Tanisha I will not say it again, will you get rid of your gum!

**Tanisha:** Alright man, chillax… Sorry Sir.

**Taylor:** Well, the way I see it yeah, religion causes war. I don't think it should exist personally. I think we'd all get along just fine if there was no religion.

**Bulldog:** *She is busy showing Queenie photos of herself.* There's one of me, and there's one of me, and there's one of me, and there's one of me.

*Girl gang is plotting and whispering. In unison they all start singing:* 'I'm so pretty, I'm so pretty and witty and' *They all look round at Gaylord* 'Gay'!

**Tanisha:** I crack me up!

**Sir:** Girls, I do not allow homophobia in my lesson. You know that.

*Teacher enters. A tall thin man. He wears a moustache and glasses.*

**Teacher:** What's all this noise? Oh, it's you.

**Tanisha:** Hi Sir.

**Teacher:** You promised me Tanisha. You promised me you would try to improve your behaviour didn't you?

**Tanisha:** It's not my fault Sir can't control the class innit! Sir's drinkin!

**All girls:** Turn round Sir, he's drinking in the classroom Sir – turn around!

**Teacher:** Turn around? So you can all stick a 'kick me' sign on my back. I don't think so. Do you take me for some sort of idiot?

**Tamara:** Yes.

**Teacher:** Haven't we had many conversations about you taking responsibility for your actions?

**Tanisha:** Yes – we've had many many conversations. Please, let's not have another one.

**Teacher:** I don't think you're taking this very seriously Tanisha.

**Tanisha:** I take life very seriously Sir. You got a buger up your nose.

Teacher: Get out…Now!

**Tanisha:** What? That was me being nice! I didn't want you to walk round all day with a buger up your nose with people making fun of you behind your back!… You can't touch me Sir. Dat's abuse… My shoulder, my shoulder. I fink you dislocated my shoulder. Ow! I can't get up.

**Tamara:** You could get done for that Sir. You know that? You can't put your hands on her like that. We could report you for child abuse.

**Tanisha:** Alcoholic! *As she is being escorted out of the classroom by teacher.*

**Teacher:** Sir, please keep your class under control. They're disturbing my lesson.

**Sir:** Right you are Sir. *Sir takes another swig as Teacher exits. Gang talk loudly among themselves. They suddenly take their voices down* *to a whisper making rude gestures joking that Tanisha is probably kissing Sir, or doing something of a sexual nature.*

**Teacher:** *From off stage.* Don't ever speak to me like that again!

*Tanisha enters and slaps Studious Girl on the back of the head as she walks to her group. As she passes the table of Queenie and Bulldog she grabs their books and throws them across the room.*

**Tanisha:** Stop disrespecting your environment.

**Queenie/Bulldog/Studious Girl:** Sir!!!

**Taylor:** Did you swallow?

**Tanisha:** Shut up! …. I'm gonna catch him right at it. Get yourself out of this one mate!

**Sir:** Tanisha, are you filming me?

**Tanisha:** Carry on. I'm gonna put it on YouTube titled 'The most boringist teacher in da whole school'.

**Sir:** Tanisha you are violating my human rights by filming me without my permission.

**Tanisha:** And you is violating my human rights by forcing me to be in dis stupid lesson. No one cares about your dumb RE lesson.

**Gaylord:** I do Sir. I'm going to be a theologian.

**Sir:** Tanisha for the last time, will you please get rid of that gum!

**Tanisha:** Fucking hell, alright! You only had to ask!

**Sir:** Come on love, write the day please, it's the 16th.

**Taqueria:** Why do you even care about this stuff Sir? It's so boring!

**Sir:** I care Taqueria because I want you to reach your full potential. I want you to live a happy fulfilled life doing what you want to do.

**Tanisha:** Ah! You're alright Sir. Bump me. He left me hanging! Fucking rude bastard!

**Sir:** Well done Gaylord. You make some very good points there. How are the meetings going?

**Gaylord:** It's really helpful Sir. I haven't gambled in five days.

**Sir:** Oh, that's brilliant Gaylord. You stick at it. And if you need someone to talk to, you know where I am.

**Gaylord:** Thanks Sir.

**Tanisha:** I got a good slut drop Sir. You wanna see?

**Sir:** No, I don't. Get on with your work.

**Girl gang:** *banging hands on table in a rhythmical fashion, chanting.* Slut drop! Slut drop! Slut drop! Slut drop! *Getting louder each time. Tanisha gets up and seductively walks up to Sir. She stands with her back to Sir ready to do a slut drop.*

**Sir:** No Tanisha! *She stops. All girls sigh in disappointment.* You're a young lady. Please act like one.

**Taqueria:** Let's show him our routine.

**Tanisha:** Oh yeah. Sir, we gonna go on X Factor. You wanna see our act?

**Sir:** No I don't. Will you please get on with your work girls.

**Tanisha:** We will in a minute Sir. Please let us just show you this.

**Sir:** Absolutely not. Will you please do as you are told!

**Tanisha:** Please Sir!… Give us very honest feedback yeah. We can handle constructive criticism, innit?

*Tanisha and Taqueria go to the centre of the classroom to show off their routine. Taqueria plays Megan Trainers 'All about the base' on her phone on loud speaker. They start to sing together very loudly doing a very bad dance routine. At the end girl gang give a standing ovation hollering, cheering and clapping as if it was great.*

**Sir:** Right. You've had your fun. Now get back to work.

**Tanisha:** But we've got a 2nd act Sir. You gotta have a 2nd act, cos sometimes they don't like the first act. Sometimes it's the 2nd act that gets you through innit.

*Taqueira plays 'Uptown Funk on her phone and they do a dance routine, with girl gang cheering them on. At the end they bow for girl gang who cheer and clap.*

**Tanisha:** Do you think we'll make it to the live final Sir?

**Sir:** No.

**Tanisha:** I'm gutted. I thought we was great! Did you ever dance when you were younger Sir?

**Sir:** Tanisha, I'm gonna have to have you removed. You're being very disruptive today.

**Tanisha:** Please don't Sir. I'll be good. I promise. Anyways, if I'm removed all this lot is gonna go, trust me, I'm doing you a favour. I'm entertaining your class. If it weren't for me, they would all be bunking right now. You should be thanking me.

*Sir leaves the room to get the headmistress. The girls whisper to each other in anticipation. All food, make up, phones are hidden. Books are open and pens are out. There is silent tension when Sir returns. By the time the head comes in, all students, except Tanisha appear to be keen to learn facing board with books open and pens in hand. Tanisha continues to be engrossed in texting someone. Headmistress enters room in silence. She walks up to Sir and whispers in his ear. He is wiping the sweat of his brow. He is shaking and swallowing pills. He looks like a desperate man.*

**Sir:** I just don't know what to do with her. I'm at my wits end. Please take her. Please, please take her. I'm begging you! *They whisper to each other. Sir leaves as Miss turns, walks towards the gang slowly and menacingly, 'Jaws' music plays in the background. The music gets louder as she approaches, and stops when she gets to the desk. Her focus is on Tanisha; Tanisha's focus is on her. Tanisha's feet are up on the desk. She is smiling. They are staring each other out as she approaches. All others are pretending to study.*

**Queenie:** Can you please take her Miss, she's so disruptive.

**Tanisha:** Shut up gay boy, before I smash your ginger fucking head in.

**Miss:** You really are a despicable human being.

**Tanisha:** I am a highly complex individual with unmet needs innit I require compassion and understanding, and…and…sympathy.

*Girls launch into 'Somewhere only we know' by Keane, starting with Tanisha. Gang join in one by one until all of them are singing.*

**Gang singing:**    Oh, sympathy, where have you gone?
                     I'm getting old, and I need something to rely on.
                     So tell me when, you gonna let me in,
                     I'm getting tired and I need somewhere to begin,
                     Oh, sympathy

*During this Miss is shouting:*

**Miss:** Stop this, stop this immediately, this is very disrespectful. How can you expect others to treat you with respect when you have no respect for other people?

**Queenie:** It's old simple thing.

**Tanisha:** What?

**Queenie:** It's old simple thing, not oh sympathy.

**Tainisha:** No it ain't.

**Queenie:** Yes it is, I know it is. I know all the lyrics. I'm a massive Keane fan.

**Tanisha:** Course you're a massive Queen fan, cos you're a queen innit?

**Queenie:** I said Keane. Is there something wrong with your ears?

**Tanisha:** It ain't simple fing, it's oh sympathy you twat.

**Taqueria:** Er, actually it is.

**Tanisha:** What?!

**Taqueria:** It's old simple thing.

**Tanisha:** No it aint!

**Taqueria:** Well Google says it is.

**Taylor:** Actually, I always knew it was old simple thing. I just didn't want to argue with you.

**Tanisha:** Well, fanks mate. You've made me look like a right knob end. And this has ruined our fing an everyfing. What we gonna do now when a teacher insults me?

**Taylor:** We can still sing a song... just get the lyrics right first, that's all.

**Miss:** Anyway, enough of all this nonsense. I'd like you to come with me please Jane.

*All girls snigger to each other.*

**Tanisha:** Shut up! It's Tanisha!

**Headmistress:** Come with me please, Tanisha.

*Tanisha is escorted out of the classroom into the exclusion room for the rest of the lesson.*

# Gary Jones

*I started writing at a time of turbulence and crisis and one should be angry about what's going on in the world. I feel it's my duty as a writer to challenge those who are corrupt, undemocratic and fuel inequality, and this is what motivates me and is reflected in some of my work. As a writer I strive to give a voice to those who are ignored, exploited and unrepresented.*

Gary Jones

# Ain't Got A Home

The city lights in all their glory
In the backstreets, it's a different story
Sitting on a kerb in a no parking zone
Why, cause I ain't got a home

The wind howls, the clouds are black
Most are immune from winter's attack
The rain comes down with a vicious lash
Sleep in a doorway in sodden trash

With the weather cold and so severe
I dig a bed under the pier
Snuggle down and start to pray
Let me survive another day

The pub spills out with an angry face
Looking into the dark scanning the place
A vulnerable soul asleep on some seating
An alcohol fuelled savage beating

Beaten so bad and left for dead
Would this have happened if I'd had a bed
Angels of mercy sooth the pain
Then patched up and on the street again

A life on the outskirts of human decay
Just get a job is what they say
They can't see past the shabby exterior
If they could it would all become clearer

Living like this is not through choice
But what can I do I have no voice
They look at me, look right through
But remember one day this could be you

# Religion

They say don't be idle
Read your bible
Yes you will learn
Or else you'll burn
Death to non believers
Humanity's deceivers
So spread and tell
Or burn in hell
But what if it wasn't there
Would anyone really care

But they're devout, devout, very devout
Spreading the word shout it out
Them of brimstone them of fire
They also have guns, guns for hire

In the wilds of religious strife
There ain't much regard for human life
They sit smugly in their pious way
Plotting extermination of their prey

But what if it wasn't there
Would anyone really care

Gary Jones

# What a Strange World

Clowns at large in dressing gowns
Dancing to the beat in far away towns
Standing by the spinning plate
Now immortalised in the Tate

The streets fill with wide eyed shoppers
At night the young and old age boppers
Ologists ask is happiness aboun'
A fella says dunno, just ask a clown

The daily saga of toothless crones
All done up and with digital phones
Striving to try and impress their mates
Desperate for boys for dinner dates

The twisted mind of a local thug
Never been loved not one hug
Spiritual freedom is not for him
But tearing people limb by limb

A fine young woman dressed in lace
Finds herself in the wrong place
The drunks they have her in their sights
Grabbing her arse in between fights

Now the clowns you know watch us close
If we resist they'll increase the dose
'Til we are so weak we cannot act
They've even got Mickey Mouse hooked on crack

There he is the man with the scars
He tells us all there's life on Mars
A closer look shows he has one arm
Yes this is cause for alarm

She closes her eyes as she drowns
There a vision of laughing clowns
They leave her to her tragic fate
She can't be saved it's all to late

Enter the gold digger in designer gear
Big blue eyes and a manic leer
Rejection letter from Big Brother
Leave well alone and run for cover

The clowns are in their background lairs
We see their shadows in our nightmares
What secrets do they know
Be sure they're never going let us go

So this is the concept that is held
Yeah you're right it's a strange old world
And as you walk in your far away town
You're only ten yards away from a clown

So through the confusion, noise and dust
Nobody realises that Britain is bust
They move to the beat in these far away towns
And worship those clowns in dressing gowns

Gary Jones

# The World's Mess

Death and destruction
In the Middle East
The political vomit
Of an imperialist feast

Dance to bullets
Revolution in Spring
People defiant
The crowds sing

Mass hypocrisy
Of the West
Spurs them on
Us they detest

In our rulers
We don't trust
We live it now
The West is bust

In the quest
To interfere
Increased danger
Some pay dear

A rusted sword
By wicked hand
A severed head
Drops into sand

In their haste
Policies of pain
Wicked revenge
Of beheadings again

We say to our leaders
Not in our name
Another head goes
Who is to blame

Religious doctrine
Hateful extreme
Our world view
Is just as obscene

The vicious hate
Of couldn't care less
But we all know
The World's a mess

# Gwyneth Edwards

*I am an historian and teacher by training and I was brought up in Wales. I am a regular member of Brighton NightWriters and my debut collection of short stories "The Sin Eaters" is out now. You can read more about the book on my website.*
*http://gwynethedwardsauthor.wordpress.com*

# The Visit

I was in my study reading and drinking port when I heard the sound of a horse's hooves. The clock struck ten - a late hour for anyone to be visiting. I edged across to the window and saw a white stallion and his rider approaching so I placed the book on my escritoire and made my way downstairs, clutching the banister for support.

As the horseman dismounted I stepped outside into the courtyard. He handed the reins to my groom.

"Make sure you give the beast a good rub down lad, he's travelled a long way," the stranger said. He was built like a scarecrow, tall and gangly with a scarred cheek. The scraping sound his boot made as it dragged against the cobbles alerted me to his limp.

"I'm sorry to inconvenience you at this late hour, Lord Wilton, but I have a message from Lady Eldon. It's urgent. I'm her clerk, Jacob Jones," he said, removing his hat.

He had come a great distance since Lady Eldon lived in Scotland. The lines on his face signalled weariness and I remembered my duty as a host. "Please come inside. You look in need of refreshment," I said, leading him to the kitchen and calling to my servant. "Bess, can you get this gentleman food and wine." She bobbed and went to do my bidding. He pulled out a scroll from his coat and handed it to me.

"Well, Jacob, once you've eaten, Bess will find you a room. You can rest here tonight." He bowed his head. "Thank you, sir."

"If this missive needs a reply I'll tell you in the next half an hour, otherwise you can depart once you've breakfasted in the morning. Good night." Moving into the hall I inched my way up the stairs and by the time I reached the top I was breathless. On returning to my study I poured myself another glass of port then broke the document's seal.

"I regret to inform you that Eldon is dead. He died from a bloody flux." - Georgiana Eldon.

My hand flew to my mouth as I read the words. Several notions flitted through my mind - I was now the sole witness and survivor.

The implications of this unnerved me and I sat up with a start, mulling things over. Since the letter did not require an immediate answer, there was time to think and I pondered over the events of that significant day.

It was thirty years since it took place, on a sultry afternoon in late June. The air was filled with the scent of roses and, remembering that aroma made me retch into my handkerchief. My three friends had been strolling with me in the woods to escape the heat which was fierce, even in the late afternoon. Francis Eldon was the first to notice the girl and he whispered as he pointed to her - "look."

We followed the direction of his finger and saw a young woman coming towards us. She was slim with long auburn hair and eyes the colour of cornflowers. Eldon indicated we should stay silent and follow him. We did as he wished and hid behind a clump of trees.

As she drew level, David Haskin moved and a twig crunched under his foot. Her eyes widened as she caught sight of us. George Farringdon was the first to break cover and give chase – the rest of us ran after him. She stood no chance and Farringdon soon trapped her. I covered my face with my hands and groaned, remembering what happened next. Farringdon threw her to the ground and unbuckled his trousers. None of us intervened. We stood and leered and, when he finished, we participated in turn. I only realised what I'd done when she crept away crying, but by then it was too late. We had not considered the consequences.

Days later when I went riding in the meadows I saw a group of men searching the surrounding woodland. I enquired what they were doing; one doffed his cap.

"Searching for the parson's niece, sir," he said.

"What's her name and what does she look like?" I asked him.

"Her name's Miriam," he replied. "She's seventeen. Her hair is red and she has blue eyes. She was due to visit her aunt but never arrived."

"Be sure to search well," I told him, giving him a handful of coins to share with the rest of the men. Their eyes fixed on the silver and they did not recognise the tell-tale blush staining my cheeks. I urged my horse on and rode off as they counted the money.

"Thank you, sir." I heard them call out.

The next day they found her - drowned in the river.

Tears filled my eyes as I recalled the moment that I was informed she was dead. It was our fault and now I was the only one left. Farringdon died first falling from his horse while hunting eight years later and Haskin followed ten years after that – dying in an accident while shooting game; and now Eldon. I would not be far behind him – my doctor had diagnosed consumption. Struggling to my feet I hobbled to the mirror to study my reflection and shuddered at the ghost looking back. The ravages of the illness were present in my hollow eyes and the extreme pallor of my face.

The clock chimed twelve. I replenished my drink and walked to the window. It was a dark and starless night; a few clouds scudded across the sky. The summer was over and rust coloured leaves covered the ground. I was glad - that season held no joy for me anymore.        Turning away from the window I drained the goblet and paced around the room. Since that time I had been unable to find peace and wondered what punishment awaited me once I departed this world. Would it be worse than this constant torment my conscience gave me?

A creak on the stair shook me from my reverie. The servants were asleep but I could hear the tread of footsteps. Hearing a soft tap at the door I went to answer it. Through the crack I glimpsed my visitor standing there holding a candle.

"What brings you here at this hour, Jacob?"

"I must speak with you," he replied. Hearing the urgency of his voice I stepped back and ushered him in to the chamber.

"What's so important that it can't wait until morning?" His eyes searched my face. "You've had some bad news?"

"Yes, Lord Eldon died."

He clasped his hands together. "Indeed. He suffered a prolonged illness but Lady Eldon expected him to recover."

"So what do you want to say?" I persisted.

"His death was not a natural one."

I grasped the arms of my chair. "What are you saying?"

Jacob's eyes bored into my head. "I know your secret."

"What secret?" I whispered. "What has this to do with his demise?"

"Everything," he said.

My mouth gaped. "How do you know this?"

"Because she was my sister and I know what you all did."

I recoiled from the look he gave me. "Who was your sister?"

His lip curled. "Miriam," he spat out.

My eyes filled with tears. "I'm sorry," I croaked.

He laughed then. "I was ten years old when you attacked her. After the ordeal she committed suicide. My uncle and aunt were more concerned about concealing the rape and self-destruction than in pursuing the perpetrators. My sister did not receive justice. They said that she drowned by accident. Over the years I heard them whispering about it when they thought I was out of earshot." He paused and straightened. "I was the only one at home when Miriam returned; her clothes were torn and bloody. She was distressed and crying that her honour had been taken. She locked her door and wouldn't let me comfort her despite my pleadings. When I went to her room at dawn the next morning it was empty."

His eyes darted to my face and I noticed the vein in his temple throbbing.

"You had been seen walking in the woods that day with your companions - on the path she always took when visiting her relatives. I vowed then to make you all pay."

"You killed Lord Eldon?" The words tumbled out of my mouth.

He smirked.

I gasped. "But he died of illness according to his wife."

"I poisoned him."

My lip quivered. "The others died by accident."

"No," he sneered. "They did not. This visit has been planned over a number of years. I learnt that Lady Eldon needed a clerk six months ago. It made everything much easier for me."

My stomach heaved. "You don't have to take revenge. I'm dying."

He chuckled. "Yes. You have the white plague. But I must be the one to dispatch you."

I looked around wildly as he moved away from me. "How can you explain my death as an accident? No one will believe you."

He grinned. "Yes they will. The disease is slow and lingering; you chose not to face the final suffering and killed yourself. Besides, you were in shock after hearing the news of your friend's death."

I choked as he took a pistol out of his pocket, but I was too weak and sank back in my chair, my forehead wet with perspiration.

He circled the room before advancing towards me. Then he cocked his pistol. My heart thudded and I closed my eyes; he was panting and his warm breath was blowing over my face. The ticking of the clock was getting louder and I grimaced and braced myself for the end. My body trembled; although my existence was wretched I feared quitting this earth to face the unknown. Moments went by but there was no other sound. When I opened my eyes he was sitting down and the firearm was resting on his lap. I coughed. My handkerchief was flecked with blood.

"Why didn't you shoot me?"

He reclined in the armchair and crossed his legs. "Since you are the last, I have decided there is another way to make amends. I want you to draw up a full confession detailing what happened. Since your span is short it will only be made public after you've gone."

"Gladly," I cried. "What happened that day has never left my memory. Not a day goes by without me regretting my actions."

I staggered up to the bureau and wrote out an account of what had transpired, emphasising my remorse and repentance for the loss of the maid's life. When the statement was complete, I signed and dated it. Jacob pursed his lips as I handed him the paper. His eyes scrutinised my admission and when he finished reading he nodded and placed the parchment inside his jacket. He strode across to the door opened it and marched out. When it closed I exhaled and brushed away the water from my eyes. Soon after, a horse whinnied in the yard. I pulled the curtain back and watched Jacob mount his steed and gallop off through the gate. When he disappeared from view I let the hanging fall. A violent pain ripped through my chest and I dropped to the ground. Through my hazy vision I saw Miriam coming towards me; she was smiling.

# Ilona Klein

*I work at the world's greatest museum by day, and I write by night. I came to Brighton 12 years ago for a semester abroad and never returned home. I can rap in German, but I suck at Pilates. This is my first publication.*

# Malted Marigolds

Marley was dead, to begin with. One more won't kill him. He pushed the whiskey tumbler past his lips and frowned as the glass clunked against his teeth. Shaking off the memory, he tried moving to the rhythm of the music, before quickly realising this was near impossible.

Startled by a vibration, he instinctively pulled out his phone. Nothing. There it was again. He could feel it rumble just above his belt. Luckily, the demanding gurgle was drowned out by a thumping bass drum. For a moment, he tried to remember when he had last eaten anything solid, but the thought was quickly dismissed.

His glass forever empty, he pushed past the smiley girl from Human Resources. "Hey, I just met Trevor's wife! Soo alike!" she hushed and gave him a conspiratorial look. Ignoring her big eyes and wide grin, he walked past miles and miles of beige food. There were three office desks covered with a rented tablecloth, and a selection of civilised drinks on top. He grabbed the bottle of Jack, a selfish contribution to a god-awful event, and took off for a smoke.

Following the red arrow below a PhotoShopped cigarette and party-hat, he could feel red-raw anger surging through his veins. Lighting a joint through gritted teeth, he inhaled deeply before holding his breath until sparks flew by. He checked his phone and found five missed calls from Zara. The fact they only ever communicated when at least one of them was canned was only a small glimpse into the complete and utter turmoil of their relationship.

Without hesitation, he sent her an "X". To her, it meant she'd won. To him, it meant nothing. To either, it meant another late night, another walk home in yesterday's clothes, another head pounding with rage. His glass now full, he put it to his lips, eyes closed, and beat his gagging throat by swallowing in three large gulps.

His co-workers inside now singing along to Mariah, he lit a cigarette with his joint and threw up over the marigolds. Potted and cared for by Nigel from Retail, their yellow and red petals curled up like spiders, protecting their bodies from harmful intruders.

Now that he knew what the end to this evening would bring, he felt even more distant from the world of Kroll, his place of work for the past six months. His stomach turned when he spotted his Line Manager, Allan, approach from the dance floor. Forcing his lips apart, he attempted a smile. "I'm glad I caught you before you disappear," Allan shouted. "Been meaning to discuss a new sales opportunity with you, big project, potentially very rewarding," he said with a wink. "If you will excuse me for one moment," Marley muttered, patted Allan's shoulder and pushed past him. A discarded cheese puff crunched under his heavy office shoe.

Back with the marigolds, he flicked through his phone contacts. So many names he couldn't put a face to, so many eager mates he couldn't identify with. Without hesitation, he dialled the worst possible number.

# Jumping the Shark

He'd usually be pulling into Brampton Primary right about now. Stopping opposite the Montebello bike shop and waiting for the school bell to ring. As the children slowly piled in, he'd always try to make sure that no one sat alone. The sight of the number 68 towards Barnstable Castle passing by was his cue to check the mirrors and close the automated doors.

As the waitress poured him another pitiful cup of coffee, he averted her questioning eyes and pushed the bulging bin liner further out of view with his shoe.

Thirty-seven years, he thought, but the most pressing concern was Vera. She mustn't find out he'd got the sack, or she'd be on the next train to Exeter.

"Less chat more speed," they'd warned him a couple of months ago. He was given a disciplinary for getting out of his seat to help an old dear up the step.

He should have seen it coming, really. Every month, he was challenged to shave off another minute between each of the 23 stops on his route from Taunton to Newton Abbot.

As he turned the key in the lock, he was relieved not to be greeted by the sound of the telly blasting out those dreadful programmes she liked. He quickly pushed through the kitchen and chucked his bags into the pantry before heading for the shower. If he made it to bed before nine, he could feign a sore back and she would leave him to rest.

The next morning, his heart sank and his scalp burned at the sound of his alarm clock. So he rose and, accompanied by his usual whistle, he pulled his uniform out of the pantry and searched for the garage keys.

Three hours, a trip to B&Q and a hose down later, and his world had been restored. As he pulled out of his driveway, he threw a broad grin at Brenda, who shielded her eyes from the sun like she couldn't believe what she saw.

He got to Tiverton Parkway five minutes early, so he waited on the double yellow with the engine on. He could feel his heart beating in his throat when he spotted the red roof of the old Uncle Gus rise like the sun in his rear-view mirror.

After it awkwardly trailed passed him, he let three cars in front before following it down this too familiar route. Rummaging around her handbag in an endless search for her wallet, Anne was queuing at her usual stop when she noticed his Mitsubishi MPV in the distance.

With a puzzled frown, she let the number 7 drive off when she thought she recognised his silhouette through the windshield. Casually, he came to a stop and climbed over the headrest to push the sliding door open.

"Did you paint that bus yourself?" Anne asked, before jumping aboard. "Yup", he nodded, and continued his journey. After collecting a sceptical-looking child from Buxton Primary, he tipped his cap and his five passengers lent back, reassured.

"So how are we all? Had a nice day?" he winked even though he had his back turned, and gave a firm nod in acknowledgement as Rita rang the bicycle bell that was clipped onto the headrest in front. "Next stop - Mutley Plain!"

# The Reader

She had just spent 45 minutes reshaping the faces and objects she saw in the sticky palm of a three-year old boy to fit in with his mother's expectations. She never lied. But some people just sat and stared, long after their allotted time had expired, until she'd fidget and stretch the truth. A failed enterprise could be veiled by embellishing prior fortune, while a bitter divorce meant a new beginning. After a rushed cigarette behind the tent, Lucinka hid the two bottles of mead she'd bought from the lion tamer behind the satin curtain before calling in the last, patiently waiting customer.

During the eleven hours she worked at the fair each day, she never engaged with anyone outside the marquee. Like a line drawn in the sand, it was a gateway into a world most people would fear.

That night, she poured today's earnings into the clay vase and let her muscles relax to the rattle of coins. Her mind clouded by mead and fanfare, she didn't notice it at first. As she straightened her rings on both hands, she caught a glimpse of her right palm, and she couldn't deny what she saw. Just above her wrist, in place of the usual forked road, was a dead end. Drawing her hand closer, she followed the deep furrow with her left index finger until she came to an abrupt halt. It wasn't so much the premature death that startled her. But according to everything she had ever read, she died two and a half years ago, just before the millennium.

Slurping a big gulp from the glass and swallowing hard, she waited for the mellow liquor to warm her chest and stomach as it trickled into her blood stream. She felt nothing. Just in front of her on the kitchen table lay a bread knife, but she wasn't stupid. How could she make a living from speaking to paying customers every day if she was dead?

With thoughts pinging around her skull like pinballs, she tried to remember the last time her neighbours complained her music was too loud, the last plane she took. It didn't add up. So far, she had been right about everything. Every crease, every dimple read correctly, this she knew because she lived in the kind of village people never left.

Like an intruder at a crime scene, she scanned the contents of her flat for evidence. Evidence of life. She yanked at her hair and winced in pain as she bit her lip. What do you search for? Apart from the local fairgoers and the girl in the corner shop, she didn't speak to anyone. But they could all see her. Couldn't they?

When she didn't show up for work the next day, nobody called. So she stopped paying rent, and crossed roads as she pleased, no longer frightened of consequences. But it wasn't long until she got bored of this new-found carelessness. When she climbed into the lion cage the following evening, nobody tried to stop her. What was the point of dying when it made no difference?

# The Long Day Called Thursday

Fifty minutes after his morning alarm rang, Walter rolled over onto his back without making a noise. The shifting weight on the mattress stirred Trudy, who gave him a quick look of annoyance, but when she noticed the blackness in his eyes, her mouth and forehead softened.

She placed one hand carefully onto his bony chest and moved her head a little closer. They lay in silence, neither of them wanting to be the first to speak.

With her patient mind miles away from their terraced house in Macclesfield, she was rolling one of the plastic buttons on his pyjamas back and forth between forefinger and thumb. So what if the thread was fraying and the button came off? It was only another menial job to add to the pile.

Staring at a new crack in the ceiling, Walter stretched his feet and toes and took a breath so slow and long that he felt too depressed to exhale. In three and a half months, he would retire. So what was the point in sending him on a training course?

Forty minutes later he was sitting in the back office next to Kevin, Store Manager of OptiFreeze, and Annabel, Health and Safety Officer from Head Office. With expressions of concern forced across their faces they absorbed instructions about their new walk-in freezer, nodding hard at each fact. It reminded Walter of a video he'd seen of a hamster doubling in size as he stuffed his ballooning face with fifteen carrot sticks.

At the end of a long day of stacking frozen goods into the freezer room, Walter pushed at the door with his shoulder but there was no give. He checked the light above his head and his ears burnt, hot and quick, before turning ice cold. It was red. The colour red had never been so alarming.

It would be at least nine hours before the cleaners would arrive the following day. Surprised at his calm, he lent across the wall and slid down to the floor. The resignation in his chest and shoulders was unchanged.

After only two minutes, he began to shiver. He couldn't remember when he last felt this tired. An hour's nap would mean an hour less waiting, he thought, and closed his heavy lidded eyes.

Dreaming of horse-drawn carriages marching down the high street, he was woken by the clattering of his teeth. His shivering was now more violent, every part of his body down to his nails and eyebrows had become frozen. His spine and bones now entangled icicles, his breathing became as shallow as a well in spring.

Every intake of icy breath felt like death. Death was spreading in his bones, freezing his blood and muscles next to racks of chicken and ribs. Submerged in delirium, Trudy emerged through muddy water and swam towards him, but before her hand could reach his stiff body, his mind spiralled up and disappeared into the shafts of the buzzing ventilator.

The next morning, Kevin arrived at the store and turned on the mains. Excited to see the freezer-room in action for the first time, he couldn't wait to switch it on. When he opened the heavy metal door and found Walter on the floor against the shelves, hugging his legs tight and his head hanging low, his first reaction was annoyance. Why take your own life on somebody else's premises?

# Jan ten Sythoff

*I am a regular member of Brighton NightWriters and am working on the second draft of my first novel 'The Celebration of Failure'.*

# Round the Table

It was good of my mother to visit yesterday, it's a long journey for a woman of eighty who's been on the NHS waiting list for a hip replacement for nearly two years, but what other option is there? I'd not spoken to anyone else in person for several weeks except, of course, the supermarket delivery people, but they change every day. Mum had brought the wildlife documentaries which my previous therapist had recommended and luckily there were a few without any African scenes. Not only would the videos help fill the day, but I also like to recall our conversations word for word, it keeps my mind entertained. She mentioned the lack of a table three times; it's awkward for her to eat from a tray on her lap. I always tell her there's not enough space, but I know she does not really believe that.

Though the studio flat is small, it still takes two hours every day to clean; I must listen to the radio at the same time, the daily chores are not enough to keep my thoughts in check. That's a lot of work, I realise that, but I spend all my time here so it's well worth it. Towards the end though, especially when I'm listening to the same news stories for the fourth time, my mind does start to wander, and I see the Serengeti, the golden plains stretching to the horizon, broken only by the occasional green of umbrella trees; I feel the relentless heat of the sun, the sweat trickling into my eyes and the endless drone of the grasshoppers. Even after all these months the same scene starts to play itself, as if it's on a constant replay in my head. Luckily, the doorbell rings, I time the arrival of the day's shopping with the end of the cleaning.

I try to watch two hours of wildlife programmes a day, it must be progress, everyone says the only way to overcome your demons is to face them. I have six subscriptions to different wildlife channels, it's enough on most days, but there's always a chance it won't be so it's good to have some DVDs as back up, or just for a change every now and again. Last week I managed to watch a whole programme about the deserts of Morocco and Algeria, it's not much but it is a start.

Mum became sad again, she said it wasn't right for a grown man not to leave his flat, she tried to persuade me to go for a drink in the café down the road, but she knows I'm the only one who can make coffee the way I like it, and there wasn't much she could say when I asked why we should pay good money for something inferior. I understand her point, of course, I don't see my friends as much as I used to but then, she doesn't understand the wonders of email and social networking. I also explained to her, once again, that I've done more travelling than most people manage in their whole lifetime. I had been working on overland tours in Latin America, South East Asia and Africa for years prior to the incident, but I've had enough of those endless open spaces, you might be able to see for miles, but that doesn't mean that you see everything, there's nowhere to hide, you are at the mercy of nature, just one insignificant piece of meat in the cycle of life.

Cooking is another key part of my day, and not surprisingly my repertoire has expanded rapidly. I've mastered soups, quiches, pies, pasta, curries (Thai and Indian), only vegetarian of course, and all sorts of egg based dishes. Recently I've set my mind on baking and made a good start with bread and some cakes, Mum was happy to take some of those, they're not really something I usually eat. If I was invited to appear on one of those cooking shows I'd probably accept, I can't imagine anything untoward happening there.

I had to stop seeing Linda, my last therapist, she refused to do home visits, but it was her own fault really: before her I was still able to walk to the shops or meet a friend in the local pub. She said we were making good progress, my anxiety was lessening and I was out of the flat almost every day. But then she suggested the trip to the zoo. We made it through the reptile enclosure, but as we approached the monkey section the waft of elephant dung brought me straight back, I don't remember what happened thereafter, I've not been out of the flat since. She did come over one time after that but refused to return, insisting that subsequent sessions be in her office, but what use is that if I can't make it out of my own front door?

Evenings are easier, there's always something to watch on the box or I allow myself a few games on the Nintendo. Reading is also good occasionally, but more often than not it does not engage my attention for very long. Tonight I settle in my comfortable chair with a steaming plate of mushroom risotto, there's a new drama starting shortly which the paper strongly recommends. I allow myself a bottle of wine two or three nights a week, I inevitably drink the whole thing in an evening, there's no point in trying to make one last and, moreover, when I have drunk a bottle I fall asleep immediately.

It's the other, sober nights that are the worst; the only way to fall asleep is to let my mind wander, and that inevitably draws me back to that day in Tanzania.

I'm sitting at the end of one of the two large collapsible tables peeling potatoes having just finished washing up after the group's lunch. There are no facilities here, they call it a campsite, but it's only a flat area with a couple of trees. Suddenly I realize I am not alone: a lioness stands, curious, not ten yards away on the other side of the table. My heart leaps, I stand up quickly clattering my chair to the ground and the animal takes a couple of paces back but continues to watch me carefully. She sniffs the air and the large, uncompromising, golden eyes stare unblinkingly. I throw all the plates, cutlery and bowls I can reach and she does retreat a few steps with low growls. I know only one thing: I must not run. My legs are like jelly, I could not even if I wanted to. Initially my shouts and gestures make her apprehensive, but only for a while, and we are left again staring at each other, and she regains some confidence. She is not five paces from me, only the table is in-between. There are some nicks in her ears and one of her front incisors is chipped, I think the animal must be quite old. But her muscles ripple under the golden fur, she is sharp and alert and those large, cold eyes do not avert themselves for an instant.

The bus had left not half an hour ago, and wouldn't be back until early evening, there's nobody else, and the mobile does not work out here. It's just the big cat and me; drips of sweat roll down my forehead and into my eyes, I must continually wipe them away. We walk round and round the table in the same direction, I must watch her constantly, and every time our eyes lock an additional shock of adrenaline joins the rest coursing through me. It goes on endlessly, her snarls and growls becoming louder as her patience thins, I have no idea how much time passes, every second is drawn out agonisingly. I pray that she will become bored and walk off at least a few tens of meters so I can find a branch to protect myself with, I've spotted one on the other side of the trees and glance over at it every now and again. My ears are begging to hear the sound of an engine, my eyes for the sight of a dust cloud, for the return of the bus. How much longer? It's impossible to know, my watch is in my rucksack, also out of reach. But what if her sisters catch up with her? Lions normally hunt in packs, hers cannot be that far away. I glance around, but what's the point, better to focus on her, if they come, there's nothing to be done.

After what seems like hours of walking around the table, always in the same direction, she starts panting and eventually flops to the floor. She is not only having a rest, but must also be thinking of alternative approaches, I have to be on my guard. She licks her front paws, scratches her neck, then slowly stands, this time approaching from the other direction and so I move away, keeping the table between, not letting her come too close, not letting myself get too far ahead, it is exhausting keeping up this level of vigil, but I have no choice. My mouth is parched, the sweat continues to trickle down my forehead, into my eyes and down my cheeks, I must have lost litres by now. Her cold, hungry stare helps to keep my wits about me, but I'm not sure for how long I can continue. She has not tried to charge me, or go under or over the table; in each case I must keep calm, not make sudden movements or seem like I am running in any way. But she just continues padding round the table and I keep the same distance from her as well as I can, it goes on and on. I am tiring and eventually reach a state in which I am fully vigilant, while at the same time overcome by a kind of dreaminess, a strange duality I have never experienced before. The sun is nowhere near the horizon, but at least the tables are now fully in shadow. The stifling heat is lessening when finally I hear a faint rumble. I will myself to stay aware, not to lose concentration now that I am nearly saved. The noise of the engine becomes louder and louder and I begin to regain hope. The lioness stops, ears erect, and glares at the approaching bus. Then our eyes lock for one last time, she snarls and walks off slowly into the long grass.

# Joe Gill

*A journalist by trade I've enjoyed writing creatively for some years. I started with an historical fantasy and I'm now on my third novel, a Middle East thriller. One of my short stories, The Caller, was shortlisted for a couple of prizes and published.*

# Biff's Gift

The thing is, said the dog to Tim, who was the only one who understood him, these stories keep popping into my head and you are the only person I can tell them to.

Why don't you tell them to other dogs, asked Tim.

I do. All the time. I think they enjoy them in a dog way. Wagging their tails and so forth. But by telling them to you, Tim, I know they will be recorded for all time.

Tim nodded. He loved the dog's stories so much that he wrote them down on a pad. His gift for understanding Biff came to him when he came out of the coma after driving his 2cv into a wall. Before that he only heard woof woof. Biff spoke to him in clear prose, with enchanting and absurd tales. There was another feature to his existence, one that made the secret of Biff's gift all the more bittersweet....

Biff began: Uncle Ebenezer no longer spoke after his stroke. Instead he sat in his armchair with a mug and a bowl. When he was thirsty he tapped the side of the mug. Tink tink tink. When he was hungry he tapped the middle of the empty bowl, which made a less pleasant clink clink until his niece Mary refilled it with stewed plums and sugar, the only thing he would eat. He never smiled, except on Sunday when all the church bells rang in the town and Mary opened the windows wide...

Tim scribbled as Biff barked then everything stopped.

Tim was sitting in a conservatory overlooking a garden surrounded by elms. It was familiar but he could not quite place it. Sitting opposite him was a dog, a mixture of German shepherd and terrier. The dog began to speak. Did you like the story, it said.

What story, replied Tim.

The one I just told you. The one you wrote down.

Tim remembered none of this. Then he looked to his side and saw a note pad and pen on a bamboo coffee table. He recognised his own scrawl. He began to read the story about a man called Ebenezer. It was strange and ended suddenly.

Is that the end of the story? he asked the dog.

Maybe. I keep the stories short Tim, otherwise you forget everything I've told you.

Really? Why?

The accident Tim.

Then Tim remembered his old 2cv and the wall. Ah yes of course. How do you know all this?

Because I was in the car with you.

Oh yes, of course you were.

Shall I tell another story?

Please do.

Get your pen and paper ready and I'll begin.

Just then Mary came into the conservatory. She smiled at Tim but he didn't smile back. He picked up his mug and spoon and clinked the top of the mug. Tink tink tink.

# Jonathan Chamberlain

*I am a published author. My published works include factual non-fiction* (The Cancer Survivor's Bible and Chinese Gods)*; narrative non-fiction* (Wordjazz for Stevie and King Hui: The man who owned all the opium in Hong Kong)*; and fiction* (The Alphabet of Vietnam and Dreams of Gold)*. My website is at www.fightingcancer.com where I offer a free download book* 'Cancer? Don't Panic!'*.*

# Green Pastures or
# Hurtling Down the Highway of Happiness

I'm from around these parts. I've been here a long time. So I know what I'm talking about. Most days I come down to have a look at all the cars hurtling by down Happiness Highway and I wonder where they're going, where they think they're going. Where they get to in the end. On and on they go.

Now, every so often, once a week at least, a person driving by will stop and ask: "How much further along is Green Pastures?" Well when they ask me that, I have to judge the situation thoughtfully for I am about to impart an inconvenient truth. Fact is, this road doesn't go to Green Pastures. I know! I know! All the road signs say this is the way to Green Pastures. And the new map they've come out with says this road goes to Green Pastures. And the engineers building the road say that, say that's where it's going. Why would they not? If folks don't come this way then there's no point building the road and if the road don't get built then the road engineers don't get paid to build it. You see where I'm going with this. So everyone will tell you that this is the road to Green Pastures. All the motels and stores along the way and the gas stations will all agree that this is the road to Green Pastures. But all you got to do is look up, look around you. That way you see there are hills with green pastures on them rising a way off to the left and more hills with green pastures off to the right, but ahead, where the road is going, there are no Green Pastures. So that's why some of them pull over and ask for directions.

So it's left to me to tell them that no, this isn't the way to Green Pastures. In truth this is the desert highway that goes nowhere. To get to Green Pastures you have to go back the way you've come; you've got to go back a distance and then take one of the small windy roads that goes away from the highway up into the hills, either to the left or to the right. In fact I always say you should drive around a lot just to see which of those little windy roads you like best.

But when I say this to the drivers who stop they get angry. They always get angry: "The map says this highway goes to Green Pastures and now you're telling me it doesn't. I think you're telling me bullshit."

Well, when they say that I just walk away. No skin off my nose they don't get to reach Green Pastures. That's their problem, no-one else's.

And sometimes they will say to me: "Sir, the reason I stopped was for you to give me hope, for you to inspire me by telling me that this is the right way, that I am on the right track. And now, wow! I can't believe it. How insensitive can you be? You've just taken all my hope and crushed it and crumpled it. You have let uncertainty take up residence in my soul. What you should have done, sir, is assure me I am on the right road. Then my heart would have sung anew and I would have driven off with new hope that soon I would reach Green Pastures. That's what you should have said to me.

And there are others who think I am just trying to trick them into deviating from the path. They say to me: "I do not wish to deviate and I do not wish to have this uncertainty tainting my thoughts. So I am going to assume that you are trying to trick me and maybe that you are planning to get a dollar or two out of me. Your purpose is mercenary, sir."

And there are others who say something like this: "Sir, can't you see I have already made up my mind to drive in this direction to Green Pastures. Your telling me I am going in the wrong direction is not useful to me."

And there are others who panic, who throw their arms up and say: "But the map says this is the right road." And they glare at me as if I am the cause of the problem.

And some come to me saying "I'm lost! I'm lost!" And I try to calm them down. I tell them I know the answer, that I can help them. But they continue to say: "I am lost! I am lost!" As if their ignorance cancels out my knowledge.

And there were times, in the early days, when I would wake up at three in the morning and ask myself: Am I mad? Everyone says the highway goes to Green Pastures. Who am I to say it doesn't? What do I know? What qualifications have I got? But then I let my mind consider the whole thing, the terrain, the ways of getting there, the direction the highway is going in, the arid wastes ahead. Then I feel comfortable again. I have that confidence again that I am right.

And if I were a patient man, I could say to them, it will not take you far out of your way to follow my directions so that you can see for yourself whether what I am telling you is true or false. And as for money, this diversion will not cost you much, and indeed this cost will be repaid tenfold in the currency of knowledge. You can go back and try one of the short windy roads and if they bring you to Green Pastures then well and good – and if they don't then you'll know I have misled you and you will be able to warn others. You will be able to say to them: "If you see an old fellow who says he knows the terrain and suggests you return and take a different road, well don't believe him sir." Yes, you will be able to say that not from prejudice or assumption but from the truth derived from your experience. And what is more, my friend, if, by following my directions, you find yourself in Green Pastures, you will be able to say: "That man told me the truth. I was lucky I stopped and asked him because everyone else was telling me lies."

Yes sir. That's what you will be able to say.

# Kathleen B. Wilson

*I've written fantasy stories all my life, much against my father's wishes, who destroyed everything I wrote. But I've found my vocation in children's literature. Even these are laced with fantasy. The story I've submitted in this anthology is a one off venture of something different. I've two books on Kindle.* 'Ghost Wood' *and* 'The Rocking Chair'.

# Who Killed Jenny Wren

In the little town of Nuttleshaw, Amelia was known as a local celebrity. She was nondescript in appearance, unique in her simplicity, and so timid, that she would jump at her own shadow. But because of her compassionate nature, she was always the first person to offer help and sympathy to anyone in need. Amelia lived alone in a house large enough to hold a big family, but she had been on her own ever since her aging parents died. With grey hair swept back into a soft bun at the nape of her neck, and skin which was remarkably unlined for a sixty year old, she was a paragon of virtue – but she had one obsession. She loved to peer into the lighted windows of other people's houses. To her it was like looking into another world. She visualised herself as being part of the family because it all looked so bright within.

On one particular evening, as dusk was falling and the street lamps were flickering on, Amelia left her house, with Macduff as her only companion. He was a Scottish terrier. They proceeded along the road. This nightly walk was a ritual. She loved this time of day when people started to turn on their lights and had not yet pulled their curtains. That's why she chose it. Progress was slow as Macduff sniffed at every tree and gate-post he passed. She had ample time to gaze within the windows. Her whole stance was relaxed. Because the road was getting darker and there were more shadows, she could observe her surroundings unnoticed. Amelia made this nightly walk last at least an hour. She wasn't in a hurry to get back to her lonely house. Macduff certainly wasn't, he was finding the smells fascinating. At one particular tree he decided it would be to his advantage to start digging.

Amelia paused, allowing him to have his way. She was happy to gaze into the lounge of Stella Masters' house, a pretty young teacher who hadn't lived in the road all that long. She always spoke to her whenever they met, and the older woman envied the younger one's bright and breezy out- look on life. Stella wasn't alone in the room. This was clearly visible through the window, because the curtains hadn't been drawn. Doctor Squires was with her. Amelia's heart gave a flutter. She admired the doctor, as did half the population of women in Nuttleshaw. He had often treated her for minor ailments at his surgery. But right now, concern flowed through Amelia and she wondered if Stella was ill, because the doctor was in her room. Her concern for the teacher intensified as she realised they were arguing. Although she couldn't hear what was being said, it was obvious Stella was becoming agitated. The doctor towered over her aggressively.

She saw Stella move away from him and stand behind an armchair, but in one lithe movement he barred her way. To Amelia's alarm, Stella struck the doctor across the face, then her arms fell limply to her sides and she backed away in the direction of the window. Doctor Squires lurched after her and in one quick movement grabbed her round the throat. Amelia forgot to breathe as she watched Stella's struggles become useless. She saw her body sag. Only his hands kept her upright. When he removed them, he stood back and watched her lifeless body fall to the floor.

Amelia stood frozen to the spot, her mouth open and her eyes wide with horror. This was a nightmare, she had to be dreaming. Happy-go-lucky Doctor Squires didn't go around killing defenceless women. At that moment the doctor looked up and out of the window. Unable to move, Amelia felt sure he saw her there as his eyes pierced the darkness. With a vicious movement the curtains were swished together, blanking out her view.

She shuddered as life began to flow through her body again. "Macduff!" she called, but her voice squeaked, she couldn't control it. Her whole body was shaking. She had just witnessed a cold blooded murder, and the murderer had seen her. She had to get away because he would be after her. He knew where she lived. With a great effort she turned away.

"Macduff. Come on old fellow. Home," she called, and pulled on the lead, dragging the reluctant dog away from the tree. At first he braced himself against her, planting all four feet firmly on the ground, but the persistent tug made him give way. Dejectedly, Macduff followed his mistress home, which took less than ten minutes.

Amelia stumbled into the hallway and slammed the front door shut. She locked it securely and shot the bolts into position, something she had not done in years. Wearily, she sank into a chair. Her breath rasped painfully in her chest. She endeavoured to fill her lungs with air. It had been a long time since she had hurried like that, all the time expecting to hear footsteps in pursuit. Macduff, with his lead trailing behind him, looked at her through reproachful eyes, wondering, in his doggie mind, why his outing had come to such an abrupt end.

A sound from the kitchen area made her feel apprehensive. With dilated eyes she looked in that direction. Fear bathed her in a cold sweat. The back door, she thought. Was it locked? Could the doctor get in that way? The sound was not repeated, so she relaxed.

Amelia took herself in hand and started to think rationally. Should she tell the police? Yes – of course. But how could she? She was not on the telephone in this house. Her father had never believed in that newfangled invention, and since he had died, she had never bothered to have it installed. To tell the police meant she had to go out in the dark. Suddenly the dark had lost its appeal. The doctor might be waiting for her outside. With shaking fingers she pulled all her curtains together so that she was isolated from the outside world. It made her feel a little better. In the kitchen she forced herself to make a cup of tea, hoping it would calm her ragged nerves. Stella Masters' face kept floating before her eyes. Amelia found it hard to think of her as dead. She was such a lively young woman. A spasm shuddered through her body and for a moment she was overcome with emotion.

Amelia's head ached really badly but she made no move to go to bed. She tried to fight off a wave of fear before it engulfed her. Suppose he climbed through an upstairs window? She wouldn't hear him moving around on the carpet. He could be anywhere in the house. She shivered in alarm. Then her eyes fell on Macduff curled up resignedly in his basket. His very presence gave her a glimmer of comfort. His hearing was excellent. He was a good guard dog. He would soon let her know if anyone broke in – that's if he was awake. Poor, Macduff. She spared a thought for him. She had ruined his evening walk.

Amelia sat at the table all night, staring into space. Sleep eluded her. When the first light of dawn crept through an opening in the curtains, she pushed herself wearily to her feet. Her head thumped and her eyes hurt. She methodically made a cup of tea, but the slice of toast she made nearly choked her. Her mind was made up. She was going to the police, although the thought of it made her tremble. It was daylight outside. The murderer wouldn't touch her now.

She picked up her cup and made a move to the sink. The door bell rang sharply. Amelia jumped so violently that the cup fell from her nervy fingers. She stood paralysed. He had come for her, she thought. The nerve of the man! Did he expect her to let him in! He was going to be unlucky. The door bell rang again, more demanding. She trembled, and ignored him by gathering up the broken crockery. On the third insistent ring a thought suddenly flashed through her mind of something she had forgotten. Her friend from the W.I. was calling on her today. Oh dear, what must she be thinking of me, leaving her on the doorstep? She made her way to the heavy front door and stopped. For a moment she stood undecided. She didn't open it, instead she called out nervously "Who's there?" Better to be safe than sorry.

The letter box suddenly snapped open, two suspicious eyes peered through the opening and a voice called. "What's the matter with you today, Amelia? Open up this door at once. It's Grace here and I'm in need of a cuppa."

On hearing the firm voice of her friend, Amelia felt some of the tension leave her. Slowly she pushed back the bolts. As the door burst open, Grace Bentley's ample form breezed through, nearly falling over Macduff who had a mind to dash out. Catching the dog by his collar, she turned and stared at her friend in consternation.

"My God, Amelia," she said bluntly, "you look awful. Are you ill?"

Amelia automatically re-bolted the front door which caused her friend to stare in surprise. Then she turned her frightened face towards Grace. "I'm fine," she lied. "I've just had a bad night."

"You look like death warmed up," said Grace, and took a firm hold of her arm and propelled her back to the kitchen. She sat her on a chair and proceeded to mix her a hot drink, to which she added some brandy. She worked with the ease of someone who was familiar with the layout of the kitchen. Once the steaming brew was put in Amelia's hand, she took a step back and surveyed her friend through narrowed eyes.

"I've known you for too many years Amelia, so stop pussy-footing around. You're far from well. So I'm going to get a doctor to you."

"No!" shrieked Amelia leaping to her feet and splashing the drink everywhere. Then seeing Grace's startled expression, she added weakly "I'm not really ill. I don't need a doctor. I'll be fine soon."

Grace placed a hand on her burning forehead and tut-tutted. "For the life of me I can't think why you haven't got a phone in this barn of a house. I'll be back in five minutes so stop arguing. You're lucky today because Doctor Squires is just up the road."

"Don't do that," panted Amelia. "I'll make an appointment later on."

"Stop fretting," said Grace, patting her arm. "It's no bother. He's just popped into Stella's house. I'll be back in a jiffy." As she made to move away her friend clutched at her. She was distraught. A wave of darkness passed over her. Her face was ashen and damp with perspiration.

"Please, no, not Doctor Squires," she pleaded. Amelia swayed and would have fallen had not Grace steadied her. Grace pushed her back into the chair and bent over her. This time her voice was gentle when she spoke. "Tell me what's wrong. Why is this house bolted and barred?"

"I...I...it's nothing. I can't...I..." Amelia paused, and then blurted out."I saw a murder. I saw Doctor Squires kill Stella Masters last night. He saw me. Do you understand. He saw me watching. He'll kill me too. He mustn't come here."

Grace didn't miss the hysteria in her voice, and she burst out laughing. Tears of merriment coursed down her face. But Amelia's horrified expression stopped her. She wiped her plump cheeks and enfolded her friend in her arms.

"Oh dear, you're so priceless. The incident should teach you a lesson, about looking into other peoples windows." She withdrew from her pocket a white card, which she pressed into Amelia's hand. Uncomprehending, the other woman read it. Grace watched the changing expressions on her face.

'TONIGHT, PLAYING AT NUTTERSHAW HALL

'Who Killed Jenny Wren'

Written by DOCTOR COLIN SQUIRES

And starring STELLA MASTERS

Amelia read no further. She was overcome with embarrassment. When at last she did speak, her voice was not so calm as usual. "I saw a rehearsal, didn't I"

Grace smiled. "You certainly did, and as you said, he saw you. He thought it might be fun to teach you a lesson about being a Peeping Tom. Incidentally, I've just left him and he's sent you this complimentary ticket to see the play. He thought you might like to see how it really ended, instead of guessing from the outside."

# Lucy Davies

*My work is woven together by fact, folklore and an insatiable reading habit! It is an exploration of that which we do not understand, of fear and ultimately of hope. You can see more of my published work at www.LucyDaviesWriting.co.uk*

# The Epilepsy Gremlin

My head is pounding and sickness whirls in my gut. I squint at the screen. I want to write. It helped before so I know it will help again. Recently I went away, across the world and then on a bit more. To soaring mountain peaks, wild lawless deserts, river canyons and caves, flat warm oceans and churning waves. I hiked, ran, swam, climbed all things which a Doctor once said to me would never be possible. That I'd need surgery to achieve. That would cause me pain. I learnt that those Doctors were wrong. That I knew my own body. That I could do more than I ever imagined.

OK, so back to the pounding head and whirling gut. Squinty eyes are go. Oh and my boobs did I mention my boobs yet? owww. yeauch. gag. throw up a bit. faint. Complain Complain. Squint and Write. Wait, don't forget REJOICE! All of this is NORMAL all of this is GOOD. All of this is JUST LIKE YOU. All of this is pregnancy. All of this is womanness. All of this is LIFE. It means I am well. I am alive.  And yet in the back of my mind, in the dark corner of the cave-of-rejoicement a figure lurks, with burning black eyes and charred flesh, with fangs dripping venom and poisonous wings that spread out trying to smother the light in the fire of rejoicement. That is the epilepsy gremlin. It claws at our happiness. Lurks in the shadows and says: "Remember, remember; listen to your friends, listen to your family, learn from woman's-wisdom. Go ahead, try. I announced none of their pregnancies, but I announced yours. I announced yours with electricity and pain. With a cold stone floor that I smashed you on. I announced yours by trying to squeeze new life from you. I roared through your flesh and ripped at your tongue. THERE ISN'T ROOM FOR ANYONE ELSE BUT ME IN YOU. You can fight me come on, I dare you. But I'll follow. I've followed for thirty years, what's nine months more?"

I hear the epilepsy-gremlin. I listen to its words. They claw round my ankles and creep up my bones. I want to take back control, don't want to let it win. So I'll tell the story of the first day we knew. The day when my moon-blood should've come. A day that the gremlin tried to steal, but I want to reclaim.

My head pounds like one of Tolkein's rock-giants is stuck inside and trying to beat its way out. I squint out of my skull. My whole body pulses with an ache. A familiar feeling that reminds me of muscles I didn't know I had. An agony that stabs into my toes, makes eyelashes seem heavy and hair like it's made of lead. A feeling I'd I hoped I'd forgotten. But it's a memory that seems burnt into my muscles, irremovable, irreplaceable, once felt forever remembered. I squint through my screaming eyelids again. A fan whirs and creaks round at me. It's hot. Very hot. Too hot for home. With an effort I lift my leaded eyes. There's a man on the bed next to me, I blink and see my husband. "Hey" he says again and in a second I see the effort it takes him to banish the worry from his eyes. I see the love and the pain and I am sorry for the pain. I know it's not my fault but it feels like my fault. And I know. I know. I know. I know, but I ask anyway. I don't know why. I ask.

"Have I had a seizure?"

He grimaces and nods, squeezes my hand "it's ok though, it's over now, you're fine. Just need to rest"

But I don't want to rest. I want, I need, to test this 'fine'. "I want a banana!" Our life comes back to me in broken pieces. The beach, a hut, semana santa, crowds, the van, like pieces of a smashed mirror each memory stabs into a new muscle. My little finger beats with pain. I force my neck up and sit up. My legs don't want to hold me, they buckle and I nearly fall but he catches me. "Whoa steady, ok there's bananas in the van"

My head reels, we walk through the sand, I thought it was still daytime but the moon is out. It hurts too much to look at it. We reach the van. I lie on the sand and throw up till there's more stars in my eyes than next to the moon. The palm trees spin overhead and I sweat on the cool sand. I thought it was over. I thought generalised tonic-clonic seizures where confined to my teenage days, student days. I thought my new so-wholesome I'm-a-grown-up-organic-Fairtrade-health-conscious-fitness -hippy life had surely cured me of this. I was wrong. The gremlin clapped his hands with glee and dug his talons in.

But I didn't know then what I know now. That that was the moment new life announced itself to me. And when I look back at the gremlin's work I choose not to see the fear and pain and horror that epilepsy is. Unlike the gremlin who is consumed by epilepsy, I am not, and I can choose. And I choose to see that all the epilepsy gremlin succeeded in doing was to surround me with more love than I've ever felt before. I choose to see respect in my husband not fear, I choose to see the kisses our friends showered me with the following day. I choose to see that through challenges comes strength and so I try with all I am to at least co-exist with the gremlin, because in fact, despite his ill-intent, he makes me stronger, makes me feel more, makes me love more, and that can only be a good thing.

# Felting a laptop case for a journalist

It arrives at my door.
Boiled and dyed, packaged and sent,
I open the sack, still earthy and warm,
Smell the heather and gorse,
Hear the wind and the dogs nipping at panicked hooves,
Take out the wool.

Lay out the fibres on my urban kitchen table,
Choose colours, consider my design,
Pull out a tuft and lay a warp, then weft,
Think of the women who came before.
Who sat in their round houses, on packed earthen floors,
Who, together, did as I now do alone.

Perhaps they too told stories,
Of sacred seeds and berries,
Of colours and cures,
Of love and death and hope.
To keep themselves dressed, babes warm,
To protect homesteads and tools of their trade.

I wet my hands and sprinkle on soap,
Just as they did before me,
Reel up in rush matting, creaking with suds
Fibres rub and shrink but I keep on rolling,
Till ancient knowledge is soaked in, and squeezed out
Every drop collected, shrunk and reused.

## Lucy Davies

Pull it out, rinse, and dry
Our Ancestor's fabric,
Made fresh and warm for you,
To wrap your words up safe in,
To link you to the past,
As you too, tell stories.

# Kamiko

*Extract from my novel 'Kamiko'. Inspired by my own experiences of chronic health conditions, it is the story of 13 year old Kamiko and her friend Ru. When Kamiko's parents mysteriously fall sick the two friends set out to save them using the ancient, magical art of Origami. Along the way Kamiko discovers that the world which she thought they inhabited is not quite as she once believed.*

I clenched my fists and released them. This was it, I could help Mum now. I heard Dad's voice in my mind's eye, 'Remember; breathe, think what you are about to do, scan your body to find the Origami source, push it out through your fingers, into the paper and begin to fold.' Then, calmly, as if it was something I did every day I followed Dad's instructions and I began to fold the most complicated dragon I'd ever seen. It was slow, painful work, after a while it seemed every fold I made was wrong and the paper was becoming soft with all my folding and unfolding. The clock on the side glowed 03:06. At 03:57 I finally began to see the shape of a dragon emerging from the paper between my hands. It was very vague, but I carried on, my intention had been clear, I'd scanned my body, found the source of worry for mum, and pushed it out through my fingers, I'd seen the orange spark energise the paper. I simply had to finish folding it.

I wriggled my fingers, and stretched my neck, it ached. I glanced at the clock, 04:20. It was really coming on, I just had the final folds on the wings to do now. I imagined Mum going into my bedroom and waking Dad up with a kiss on his cheek. That was a good thought. I smiled and folded the last of the dragon spines, I was half way there! I'd made another Origami piece! Full of hope, I looked at the instructions.

In a split second I knew I'd failed. Where the instructions were yawned a black hole, a swirling vortex of blue scales sucked me in, I felt my stomach flip and again a pair of orange eyes locked onto mine. Then nothingness embraced me. A chair... the table above me and... books far too close... where am I... a cushion.... cold feet...

my head. Ouch, I put a hand to my head and felt a raw bruise. I blinked my eyes, I seemed to be on the floor. Moaning I sat up. My body ached like before but this time I was on my own. What had happened? My face was sticky. I wondered how long I'd been out this time? Slowly I righted the chair and pulled myself up onto it. Memories came back in bits, the instructions, a paper dragon, mum's transparency. The orange eyes. What was that about I wondered? Was it just light? Or maybe there was someone there? Watching? Either way it didn't matter, I'd failed. Mum! I leapt up and ran upstairs, hoping against hope she'd still be there. I opened the door and saw her ghostlike form on the bed. Still there. I breathed more easily and went back downstairs.

Better leave it to Dad. No need for him to know about this. I looked at the clock - 06:15. He'd be up soon. Groggily I tidied the paper and balled up the origami dragon I'd attempted, stuffing it into my pyjama pocket. I returned upstairs. It was past 6am now, Dad'll want to start I thought. I'll go and wake him.

I knocked gently, there was no answer so I pushed open the door and leant against it. Dad was on the bed. He was bright paper-white. Just like Mum. His hair, his face, even the duvet covering him had turned white. My legs gave way and I slipped slowly down the door "Dad?" I whispered "Dad?!" This time there was no one else to see him but me. I was alone. This time, there was no one to blame. This time, it was surely my fault.

The bedside light was on and in the yellow light I burst into sobs, but no tears fell. I couldn't look away. I felt numbness clawing at me. I dragged my heavy body to the corner of the bed 'Dad?' I croaked. He obviously couldn't reply. I checked his chest, it was rising and falling. I tucked the blanket around him. "Dad! Wake up!" I said. I knew it was useless. Fear wrapped around me, I didn't know what to do. A feeling of utter desolation rose up through the cottage, I stuffed my fist into my mouth and bit down so hard on my knuckle I tasted blood. I could not cry. I had to pull myself together and think. Somehow the origami dragon I'd created had made Dad sick too instead of healing mum. I must've made a mistake. Mistake. Mistake. The word rolled around my mind till I thought I might go mad with it. I shook my head. Mum! I rushed into the other room, she was there, faint, but there. I sat down on the bed next to her. Then the tears came. They rose up like a tsunami and I was glad that no one could see me. I sobbed into the pillow next to Mum till my throat was raw.

My head pounded, for a mini-second I imagined I was in the van, I heard Mum and Dad laughing, then I blinked and the truth sunk in. I sat up. Grey morning light filtered in through the curtains. Suddenly I couldn't bear to be in the house any longer. I needed to make a plan. I grabbed up my jeans and hoodie and pulled them over my pyjamas. Avoiding looking at Mum, I grabbed the borrowed skateboard and headed away up the now familiar road to town.

I guess other people other 'normal' people had friends to call on, maybe even family, but my grandparents where dead, there were no siblings, no cousins, no friendly Auntie who sent me birthday cards, no god-parents or distant relatives. It had never occurred to me to think about what might happen if Mum and Dad were both gone... but now, I tried to scrub the panic from my mind. This wasn't all quite true. I did have a friend. A new friend, Ru, he was new, but he was kind. He'd lent me his board and... I tried to justify it to myself. I needed someone else. I couldn't work out what to do. I wiped away a tear that leaked down my face. Ru wasn't going to see me cry, that was for sure! I needed help. I needed someone else. Ru was the only someone I knew so it'd have to be him.

I skated to the park as quickly as I could, swerving around some morning carol singers, who yelped as I sped past. As soon as I arrived I could see that the park was deserted. Typical. The one time I really needed someone, it was empty. I tried not to think about Mum and Dad but images of them, white and transparent kept bursting into my mind. I wondered how long Mum would... I stopped the thought and tried to distract myself by skating into the bowl. If I couldn't find Ru, then what? I was concentrating on a turn, when I heard him.

"Hey Kam!" Ru called, "You're early" I skated up to him. Jumped off my board and impulsively hugged him tightly, burying my face in his neck, he smelt of soap and salt of toothpaste and must on his hoodie. Surprised he hugged me back. It was the first time we hugged. I shut my eyes and held on a moment too long. It would've been nice to stay in that hug and not face the conversation I knew would come. "Hey, what's that for? You OK?" he asked and I felt the tip of my ears burn. My tummy lurched, full of sickening butterflies. "Where are the others?" I asked.

"Not here yet, it's still pretty early."

"I need some help Ru" I had to get it out, my heart pounded and I felt the blood rush to my head. "Please" I added.

"Sure, what's up?"

I fought for words to explain, there was so much. I settled for the simplest, most believable "my parents are sick."

"How sick? In hospital sick?"

"No, at home."

"Well did you call a doctor?"

"I can't. It's not the kind of sick a doctor helps with."

Ru looked completely confused, I don't know what he was thinking, I didn't have time to wonder, and I just wanted him to do something. Anything. Tell me what to do.

"OK but then how are they sick?" I didn't know how to explain. There was only one choice, I'd have to show him. Tell him the whole story.

"I can't explain..." my voice faltered "but, er, I can show you. Can you come?"

"Now?"

"Yes, now."

"OK" Ru nodded, "we can skate later." I hardly listened. Right now I only cared about how fast the skateboards could get us home.

I turned and skated off fast, I heard Ru's wheels following behind me. I was glad the wind made my eyes water. I hoped that when I reached the house, somehow the story would just fall out and maybe then Ru would just, somehow, magically believe me and know what to do. Maybe. Stopping by the garden gate, I indicated the way up to the cottage. It had started to rain and we hurried over the lawn to the door. "Nice place," said Ru. I didn't answer, I suppose it was. I hadn't really thought about it, maybe if Mum and Dad had been OK I'd have thought that too but as it was Mum had been white since we'd been here and I was starting to hate the cloying pink walls.

As we arrived I felt the blood drain from my face. "What if?" I started trembling. I stopped outside the front door. Trying to hold in the tears. Mentally telling myself to get it together. "Hey, hey Kam, it's OK. I'm here. Come on, let's go in."

With an effort I steeled myself. "Come on" Ru said again. I opened the door, shaking droplets of rain onto the doormat. At least I was home now. Near them. All of a sudden Ru, looked nervous, "Perhaps I should wait here and you go and see your parents?" he said. "Isn't it a bit - er - rude, they've never met me, if they're not well won't they not feel like meeting a stranger?"

I wished that I could say yes, he should wait. That would've been better, it would've meant they would've been better.

Lucy Davies

# Learning your name

It has taken a long time to learn your name.
You stick in my throat and close up my airways,
You wake me at night, screeching through my veins,
You curl soft fingers into fists,
Pound the blood into my head so fast I can't hear or think, feel or move,
You turn the world red and black and strike across my sky.

I met you first when I was so new and fresh I could hardly see
Which way was up and which was down I didn't know
I knew you were wrong. Something not OK.
I knew you couldn't be let out.

You scared me. I saw you spill over,
A broken plate, a slammed door,
Your forked tail whipping past, just out of sight,
I saw your shadow on the stairs,
At the foot of the bed and in the window.
Your artillery astounded me.

Shells and rockets, short and long range weapons,
Bombs and bangs. Knives and cut glass.
I built defences as best I could...
You always had more...
You came for me on high days and holidays
You came for me on memory-makers, remember-forevers
and hold-in-hearters,

You clawed out my eyes and scorched my soul.
Your tears left acid on my cheeks
The plate you broke lodged in my throat for eternity

Every ragged breath a reminder of your victory
Porcelain crumbs and door splinters swept up by others,
Decorate my lungs,
A shattered butter-dish sits over my heart
And a bent doorknob's burnt into my skin
I looked for you, I did.

Under rocks, with tooth and nail
I searched, in nooks and crannies
Till my sweat poured and blood flowed.
Till I looked in the eyes of Agony and finally, finally, I saw you.

You are Anger.
That is all. Now I know your name.
I've seen where you hide and what you do,
I know your secrets.
I know how you can split yourself into pieces buried so deep, no
spade can reach you,
I know what can.
Now I know your name, I can look you in the face.
Now I know your name, I can begin again

# Malcolm A Beith

*I have been writing for pleasure on and off across many years. Since joining Brighton NightWriters I have been experimenting with the short story format, while working on my novel.*

# A Fortune in a Teacup

Mavis Fletcher sat in her old threadbare armchair and worried about the future. The rent was due next week, and she didn't know where she was going to find the money. Old Mr Harrison, her landlord, was a decent enough sort. He'd helped her out in the past, and she knew he wouldn't press her this time either, but next month things would be different. Mr Harrison was due to have a heart attack in two weeks' time, on the seventeenth to be precise. It would be his third, and this time he wasn't going to make it, poor old soul.

And poor her, with the prospect of a new landlord, one who hadn't known her for 20 years and was sympathetic to her position. She'd owe a thousand pounds by next month, and she had no idea how she would raise it.

The problem was, she hadn't picked up a new client in years, and the ones she had were getting old. One by one they were gradually dying off, like poor Mr Harrison. Today, for example, she only had one appointment, her regular Tuesday three o'clock, Connie Arkwright. Thank goodness for Connie. She wasn't exactly young herself, but she had another seventeen years in her, Mavis knew.

But what Mavis really needed was some new customers. The trouble was, people these days just didn't believe in fortune telling the way they used to. It was the same with religion. People weren't prepared to believe in *mystery* any more. Mavis blamed reality TV.

There had been a time, oh, years ago, when a steady stream of customers had found their way to her door. But times changed, and so did fashions, even in the supernatural. Nowadays people wanted mediums and seances. They wanted to talk to the dead! Mavis didn't hold with that kind of thing.

'My gift doesn't run in that direction,' she would tell prospective clients, 'So don't go asking me to contact your dearly departed. Futures is what I do.'

No, Mavis didn't like the idea of talking with the dead. It didn't feel right and, frankly, it gave her the willies. Besides, you couldn't be sure what they'd say. Imagine if your late hubbie told you he was burning in hellfire for all eternity. It would be upsetting wouldn't it!

Mavis didn't believe in upsetting people.

They came to her for hope. Hope for a better future. And she tried to give it to them, but sometimes it was hard. For most people, life *wasn't* full of tall dark strangers and unexpected inheritances. For most people, tomorrow was likely to be much the same as today. And for the sort of person who sought the help of a fortune teller, today was usually pretty miserable.

Oh, Mavis knew there were people out there with wonderful, glowing futures, futures full of glamour and excitement, big houses and yachts and things like that. But that sort of person was too busy making that wonderful future happen to bother with fortune telling. They didn't expect Fate to provide the good things. They just went out and got them for themselves.

The people who came to Mavis, people like Connie, led humdrum lives, and it was a struggle sometimes to find anything worth mentioning. 'You're going to get a good deal on PG Tips this week at Asda,' wasn't the sort of thing people wanted to hear.

But Mavis never made stuff up. She didn't hold with lying. It was, she felt, a betrayal of her gift. So she would find some small event, a letter from a grandchild perhaps, and wrap it up in a bit of mystery. 'You will receive a communication from a distant loved one,' that sort of thing. Old customers like Connie understood the limitations, and were satisfied.

It was funny, Mavis thought now. Even Connie, who had been coming to her for years, only half -believed in her gift. And Mavis was careful to keep it that way. Every now and again, she'd throw in some little inaccuracy - not a lie, not exactly - just something out of place, a wrong date perhaps, or a chance meeting with an old acquaintance that didn't occur.

She probably needn't have bothered. People like Connie never really thought about things very deeply, or she'd have realised that, if Mavis could see her receiving a letter from her grandchild, she could also see her standing in her knickers brushing her teeth in the morning, or making desultory love with her husband on a Friday night.

It didn't do to let people think too deeply.

But young people these days didn't want to hear about letters from relatives. They didn't even want to meet tall dark strangers. They wanted bigger things; fame, fortune, drama.

Mavis didn't hold with drama. At least, she didn't hold with *telling* people about drama.

Many was the time she'd read the leaves and seen something nasty in them, lying in wait behind the months and years. Cancer, maybe, or a heart attack. She never told. It wasn't her job to go telling people they were going to die, was it? It wasn't as though she could do anything about it. She wasn't a doctor. No, if they were going to have a heart attack, they'd find out soon enough without her help, thank you very much. Just like poor old Mr Harrison.

She sighed. From where she sat, there wasn't much future in fortune telling.

The knock on her door took her by surprise. It was barely two o'clock. Connie had never been early before. She opened the door and looked enquiringly at the young woman standing on her doorstep. In one quick glance she took in the tiny mini skirt, the revealing halter top, the fish net stockings and the ridiculously high heels. Ah, she thought, one of *those*. Over the years, she had counted quite a few prostitutes in her clientele. They were mostly simple girls looking for a ray of hope, an indication that, somehow, one day, they would escape their dreadful lives. Mavis tried to give them comfort where she could.

'Hello,' the woman said. 'Are you...I mean is this the right house...that is... I was told...'

'Come in dear,' Mavis said kindly. 'Who gave you my name?'

'Just... someone I met at a party,' the woman said. 'Oh, I'm sorry. My name is Felicity. You're Mavis, is that right?'

'That's me,' Mavis agreed. 'Sit down at the table and I'll put the kettle on.'

As she made the tea, Mavis took a second look at the girl. Pretty little thing, she thought, under all that silly make up. It looked as though someone had given her a couple of black eyes, and the lipstick...well, only one sort of woman would wear that colour! But it wasn't her place to judge. Who knew what the poor girl's story might be. Mavis certainly didn't. It didn't work that way. She could only see the future, never the past.

'Right then,' she said when the girl had nervously drunk the proffered cup. 'Let's see what we can see.' She made sure to touch the girl's hand as she took the cup from her, just a brush of her fingertips but it was enough. In truth, Mavis didn't read the future in tea leaves. They were just a prop. All she needed was to touch that person, and her mind would begin to form images. Usually the images were hazy, incomplete, but on occasion, they could be startlingly clear.

As the young girl watched anxiously, Mavis gazed unseeingly at the leaves and let her mind focus.

Instantly an image formed. An old man lay in an operating theatre, his chest clamped wide open as surgeons worked on him.

'Your father is ill,' she said, and the girl gave a little gasp. 'His heart,' Mavis went on. 'They're going to operate on him...let's see...next Tuesday.'

The girl had her fist in her mouth and tears were beginning to gleam in her eyes. Mavis fast forwarded a little. 'He's going to be all right,' she told the girl with satisfaction. 'The operation will be a success.'

The girl gave a little moan and tears flowed down her cheeks, streaked with black mascara.

'There, there, dear,' Mavis said distractedly. Another image had formed in her mind and she was trying to make sense of it. It was the same girl, the one who sat before her, but without the silly makeup. She looked fresh and clean and happy. She was in the garden of a fine house, and, somehow, Mavis knew it was *her* house. Her clothes were expensive and tasteful. Another image followed - the girl driving a beautiful, sleek, red car, though Mavis had no idea of the make. Again though, she was quite certain it was the girl's car.

'You're going to come into some money,' she told the girl, who stopped sniffling and looked at her quizzically. 'Quite a lot of money,' Mavis added.

She was desperately searching for a clue as to how the girl's circumstances would change, but nothing was coming to her. All she could see were snatches of her future life; a party aboard a yacht, an elegant ball with the girl in a beautiful gown. And then it came to her. An image, as clear as day, of the girl buying a lottery ticket! In the background she could just make out a sign that read, 'This week's grand prize, seventy two million.' She recognised the amount! She'd seen that sign herself. Everyone was talking about it - the biggest prize there'd ever been.

And this girl was going to win it!

Well, that was nice, she thought. The poor girl deserved a bit of luck. Maybe she should charge her double, for telling her the good news. She could certainly afford it, if not now, then in a very short while. But no, that wasn't right. It wasn't her place to share the girl's good fortune, was it? That was when the idea came to her, all of a sudden, in a flash of inspiration. It took her breath away, the audacity of it. She couldn't, could she?

'You're going to win the lottery,' Mavis told her carefully.

The girl looked surprised. 'I am? But I don't do the lottery.'

'This time you will,' Mavis said with more conviction. 'And you're going to win! But only if you do what I say.'

Her mind was working very fast now. She rose quickly from the table and crossed the room to the old Welsh dresser that had been her mother's. From the top drawer she took a purse and from the purse she took a two pound coin. Then she found an envelope and wrote her name and address on the front. Returning to the table she placed the coin in front of the girl.

'This is what you must do,' she said. 'You must buy two tickets for the lottery this week, you understand? There's the money for one. You must pay for the other yourself.' She paused, to make sure she had the girl's full attention. 'But this is the really important part. You must buy two separate tickets with the *same* numbers on each. That's very important. And then you send one of the tickets to me.'

The girl looked doubtful. 'I don't know...' she said.

'You must!' Mavis insisted. 'It's the only way it will work!'

The girl thought for a moment. 'You say my father will be all right?'

'Yes, yes,' Mavis said. 'He's going to have something called a...a quadruple bypass, I think it was...and the operation will be a complete success. He will live for years and years.'

The girl seemed to make up her mind. 'All right,' she said, pocketing the coin. 'I will.'

Mavis searched the girl's face, desperate to know whether she was telling the truth. Then she closed her eyes and concentrated hard. Yes! She could see it. She could see the girl putting the ticket in the envelope and posting it. She wished she could see herself opening it, but it didn't work that way.

When the girl had gone, Mavis made herself a cup of coffee, which she much preferred to tea, and sat in her old, worn armchair to dream of how she would spend her share of the winnings.

Outside, the girl climbed into a car which was sitting at the kerb with its engine running.

'That didn't take long,' the driver said. 'How'd it go?'

'It was....very peculiar,' the girl said hesitantly. 'She told me daddy is going to be okay.'

The man looked sceptical. 'Well...that's good then,' he said kindly, but the doubt in his voice was evident.

'No! It wasn't like that,' the girl cried. 'I didn't even tell her he was sick. *She* told me. She said he's due to have a quadruple bypass on Tuesday. How could she know that? And she said the operation would be a complete success.'

The man blew out a puff of breath. 'Well...' he said uncertainly.

'But there's something else,' the girl interrupted. 'I have to buy a lottery ticket. Two actually.'

The man looked surprised. 'Really? Why on earth...?'

'I don't know. But the old lady said I had to. She said I would win.'

'Felicity,' the man said kindly, 'I really don't think...'

'I know how it sounds, Charles,' she said. 'But she said Daddy would be all right. I don't want to jinx it. Here! Pull up over there, next to that newsagent.'

'You're really going to buy a ticket?' the man asked incredulously.

'Why not?' the girl asked. 'The old lady even gave me the money for it.'

A few minutes later she climbed back into the car. She looked much happier.

'All done?' the man asked.

The girl nodded. 'It's in the mail,' she said. 'Now I can relax.'

'Good,' the man said. 'It's nice to see you smile.'

The girl looked at him then, as though seeing him for the first time. 'The dog collar suits you,' she said.

The man stuck a finger in the collar and tugged. 'Perhaps,' he said, 'but it's damned uncomfortable. I'd much rather be wearing my dinner jacket. It's going to be a long and tiresome evening. Vicars and Tarts. I ask you. Couldn't Marjorie come up with something more original than that?'

He put the Bentley in gear and the big car purred as it pulled away from the kerb and swept off into the night.

A week later, Felicity parked her little Ferrari outside the old lady's house. Quickly, she entered the dark hallway and climbed the bare stairs to the second floor. It was strange, she thought. The old lady had seemed so sure. Felicity had found herself, against all common sense, believing she really could see the future! It was ridiculous, of course. But Daddy had survived the operation, as predicted, and was recovering well. That was the important thing. She had been so relieved, and so grateful, she'd actually checked the lottery ticket to find out if she'd won.

She hadn't, of course.

Charles had laughed at her, but he wasn't being unkind. They were just both so relieved. It was good to be able to laugh again. And they certainly didn't need the money. They had enough to last ten lifetimes. She realised now just how desperate she had felt. Desperate enough to visit a fortune teller!

Outside the old lady's apartment, she bent and slipped an envelope under the door, before quietly making her way back downstairs.

Charles didn't know she'd come. If she told him, he be cross. But somehow, she felt she owed the old lady something. She couldn't justify it. As Charles had been quick to point out, the old dear had been right about one thing and wrong about the other. That made her right fifty percent of the time, which was exactly what you'd expect if she were just guessing.

But still...

In the envelope was a note that said simply, 'Thank you', and a cheque for one thousand pounds. She didn't know why, but somehow, that seemed to be just the right amount.

# Marita Wild

*I am a brilliant writer. If you don't believe me read my book 'Monkey On My Roof', a mixture of fact and fiction about India, which for a Liverpool girl who has worked as a clerk, shop assistant, mannequin, and watch repairer was an experience not to be missed.*

# Just One Of Those Things

Singing *It Was Just One of Those Things* is not the most diplomatic thing a guy can do after screwing his girlfriend to the mattress then ditching her before the condom has had a chance to crinkle. Not that they'd done any screwing; there had been no need for post-coital cigarettes. No coital, and no post. The postman hadn't cum.

'Want to try again?' Helen asked.

Justin stubbed his cigarette out, 'Fuck it! I've had enough. You and me are finished.'

'Well… that was unexpected.'

'I'm not joking. It's over.'

Helen followed him into the bathroom, and opened the bathroom cabinet, a fingernail was broken and needed trimming, 'So that's it then! Wham, Bam, no thank you Mam.'

'Oh fuck off!'

'It isn't my fault you can't get it up,' she said and picked up the nail scissors, 'I'm usually the one who finishes things.'

'Not this time. Shit happens; get used to it,' he stepped into the bathtub, and pulled the shower curtains across, 'You should get a shower stall.'

'Don't talk to me about shower stalls! Talk to me about why you want to finish it.'

'I've met someone else,' he said through the shower curtains, 'someone who doesn't need a boob job.'

'That's a bit rich coming from a musician with a tiny organ. Not particularly well-endowed are you.'

'Yeah, well I didn't think I'd be playing it in a cathedral!'

'You bastard!'

'Yes I am rather, aren't I?' he said, and began to sing, *It was just one of those things. Just one of those crazy flings…"*

That was it: The last straw, the nail in his coffin, bags all packed and ready to go.

Helen pulled the shower curtain across and threw the nail scissors at him.

There was a cry, not quite a scream from the bathtub; the sort of cry which couldn't be ignored. Justin was sliding slowly down the tiled wall with the scissors sticking out of his neck.

'What have you done?' he whispered, the look of shock on his face mirroring hers. Blood spurted like a fountain as he pulled the scissors out.

 Helen jumped into the bathtub, 'Oh God! Oh God! I didn't mean to do that!'

She knelt down beside him and pushed her fingers against the wound. So much blood! On him, on her, on the tiles, on the shower curtains! How could a person have so much blood?

She looked at Justin, in disbelief; how could a tiny pair of nail scissors cause so much damage? But Justin was dead, deader than anyone she'd ever seen before.

What a shame; as lays go he hadn't been so bad; not the best, but not the worst either.

What to do? What to do?  Too late for an ambulance. An ambulance wouldn't be any good.

I could call the police. Tell them he was in the shower cutting his toenails? They'll never believe it! Who in their right mind would believe Justin mistook his jugular vein for his big toe? I'd be standing in the dock looking at twenty years in Holloway. Could a good solicitor get me off? No chance! Even if he did get me off. Even if I were to be acquitted, there'd be all the hassle of reporters and camera crews. The News of the World would have a field day. A bigger scandal than Jimmy Savile! I'd lose my job for sure. The Beeb wouldn't tolerate one of their news presenters standing trial for the murder of her pop star lover.

The shower was still running, Helen reached up and turned it off.

'Damn it: my two hundred and twenty pound hair-do is ruined,' she said to Justin's dead face, 'now I'll have to go to the hairdressers again!'

Helen kicked his arm: 'Why should I go to prison because of a second rate guitarist in a third rate pop band.

I'll get rid of him, that's what I'll do. A couple of bin bags and the wheelbarrow should do it. His bottom half can go in one bin bag, and his top half in another. It's high tide tonight. I can shove him in the wheelbarrow and tip him into the sea.

Grasping Justin's arm she got out of the bathtub, and made to pull him out.

Shit! He's a dead weight! How will I get him in to the wheelbarrow?

That's it! The electric jigsaw in the cupboard!

Four hours later, the jigsaw was back in the cupboard, the tiles scrubbed clean, and the bin bags stowed in the wheelbarrow.

Helen shampooed the blood from her hair and gave a last look around the bathroom.

Oh damn I've left his fingers and toes on the floor! They should be in the wheelbarrow with the rest of him. Wouldn't do to forget them.

*

The wheelbarrow squeaked softly as she pushed it along the boardwalk, Tomorrow morning, Helen thought, I'll put his clothes in a bin bag. They can go to a Charity Shop. Then there are the shower curtains. Mustn't forget the shower curtains! Justin was right; I should get a shower stall fitted.

She tipped the contents of the barrow into the English Channel, and smiled: No-one can find him now! The police can investigate, and the media speculate as much as they like; in a couple of weeks, no one will give a damn about the disappearance of a guitarist in a boy band.

The barrow was easier to push now that it was empty, but a small plastic sandwich bag remained in the bottom. Helen stared at the bag; damn I've forgotten his fingers and toes after all! Oh well, they can go in the fridge. I'll go to the pier and feed them to the seagulls tomorrow

The voice from behind her came as a surprise, 'Allo. Allo. Allo. What's nice a girl like you doing in a place like this in the middle of the night?'

Helen turned slowly, 'Oh hello officer! I've been taking some rubbish to the dump.'

The police officer looked into the wheelbarrow, where at the bottom, Justin's fingers and toes were clearly visible in the transparent sandwich bag, 'What the fuck…'

Oh well shit happens.

On the other hand, there was another roll of bin bags in the kitchen drawer…

Marita Wild

# My New Printer

Last month I bought a new printer
All shiny and new in a box,
It came with instructions and CD
There shouldn't have been any shocks.
The man in the shop said: "Its magic
And ever so user friendly.
Just plug it in, set it up and get going
You'll marvel at its simplicity.
The panel has many fine programmes,
Image matching and colour control
There's a button that turns on and off
In case you get into a hole."

I followed the instructions he gave me
So why don't the images match?
And why when I only want one print
Do I get thirty-two in the batch?
Each one like a Picasso painting
With a nose where the eyes should have been
The colours all mixed up and manky
Blues and reds where they ought to be green
I'm buried in mountains of paper
My photos have all been a flop
I can't get the hang of this printer
So I'm sending it back to the shop

# The Metal Workers Tale

It was a plain house, tall, with whitewashed walls, and a short drive leading to a courtyard. No crystal castle this. Not a grand house as houses go, but no mean one either. The road was hot and dusty and I felt no hesitation in riding up the drive to ask for water for my horse. The man in the courtyard was plain like the house, with a bulky body and a crippled leg, his face only saved from ugliness by a merry smile, and the laugh lines around his eyes. A surprisingly happy face. So much so, that as I led my horse to the water trough I found myself remarking how rare it was to see a man looking so contented.

He laughed. 'It wasn't always so. Nowadays I have no reason to be unhappy. Not so long ago I was full of rage.'

Then he offered me a glass of wine and told me his story.

At six years of age, I awoke and heard my parents talking in the courtyard below. They were talking about me. I got out of bed and limped to the window.

My mother saw me there; she turned to my father, 'Get that thing out of my sight! It disgusts me.'

'Have you no love for him? We made him together,' my father said.

And my mother, so faultless in her patrician beauty, demanding perfection in everything around her, answered 'I can't bear to look at him. Send him away husband or I'll do something we will both regret.'

It's harsh to be so despised by one's mother.

I was sent away to live in the valley with my Grandmothe, whose unconditional love didn't demand perfection from its object.

'Come and give your Granny a kiss Jarvis,' she'd call whenever I passed her chair.

Then she'd sit me on her knee to tell me the old stories, sing me the old songs, and wipe my tears when I cried with grief. Three times a week she took me to the priest for instruction; because after all I was my father's son and my father was an important man.

Noticing that I loved to work with metal, Grandmother arranged for me to have lessons with a master artisan. Her praise when I surpassed his skills went a long way to mending my self-esteem, and her pleasure in the gifts I made gave me the confidence to create beautiful objects.

'He can't help being clumsy,' she'd tell her cronies if I knocked a goblet over in passing. 'It's the lameness that makes him awkward.'

Grandmother persuaded me to make baubles for her friends, bracelets to encircle skinny wrists, necklaces to adorn wrinkled throats. She smiled slyly at their surprised delight when I offered the trinkets, 'See! He is not so clumsy. When Jarvis works the metal he is all grace and beauty.'

The first piece of jewellery I made was for a handmaiden, a slave Grandmother had brought home from the market place to wait on me and be my companion.

Alyssa and I were the same age, from six to sixteen we were seldom apart. Darkly beautiful, with golden skin like warm velvet and eyes deep pools of midnight darkness, Alyssa's black curls tumbled abundantly around a perfect heart shaped face. Her beauty, contrasting so sharply with my ugliness, affected me deeply.

I made her a heavy gold chain and a pendant of red gold, a simple disc showing the rays of the sun on one side and a crescent moon on the other.

'Jarvis! It's beautiful,' she said, 'I'll never take it off.'

True to her word, she never did; she kept it on even when, more skilled in the art of jewellery making, I offered to exchange it for something finer, something perfect.

'No Jarvis! It is already perfect,' she said.

Then my parents came to visit.

My father was jovial and loving, exclaiming at how tall I'd grown, praising my achievements, drinking wine with me, teaching me how to get drunk without falling over, and roaring with laughter and pride when I managed to stay on my feet longer than he'd expected. 'You're a chip off the old block my son.' I could feel his love warming me.

My mother shrugged as she took the jewellery I'd made her, passing it to her slaves and contemplating the warmth between Alyssa and me with quiet distaste.

Feeling my mother's icy contempt I felt no surprise when she left taking Alyssa with her. 'I need a new slave, and this one pleases me,' she told Grandmother. 'Besides, Jarvis and she are becoming close. It would be wise to separate them.'

But Mother couldn't keep me away from the mountain forever. My deformity had put off the moment but I had reached twenty and the time was long overdue for me to fulfil the manhood ritual. Father called me home,

In the courtyard my parents were overseeing the servants.

Father looked up, and seeing me, his strong handsome face lit up with a smile before he made the shooing motion with his hands that told me to go in. Mother turned away, I'd become used to seeing that weary expression of dislike whenever she saw me but now it didn't bother me. Alyssa that most beautiful of handmaidens was calling 'Come Jarvis, time to get ready.'

She stood by the bath, long black hair hanging to her hips, the pendant I had made swinging to her waist, the heavy gold chain snaking cunningly between her bare breasts, holding the gold disc suspended just above her navel. She was even more beautiful than I remembered.

When I stepped into the bath she washed me carefully, but then her cool slim fingers wound around my shaft, and it was as if the heat from all the molten metal I had ever worked with had collected there, in that spot, and I gasped her name with delight.

'Jarvis,' she said, as she looked down. Her eyes had never turned away from my crippled leg the way that other eyes did, Alyssa's eyes had never made me feel ugly and awkward. But it wasn't my leg she was looking at. And I wasn't crippled there.

'Jarvis,' she said again, and I surged out of the bath.

It was the first time for both of us, and I knew that if it never happened again it would be enough. Afterwards, she bathed me once more and rubbed oils into my body before dressing me in my robes.

'Your name will be called today,' she said as she braided my hair, 'but it won't matter now if you aren't strong enough to withstand the ceremony. Today you have proved yourself a man.'

I grabbed her around the waist and swung her around. 'I feel strong enough to withstand a hundred ceremonies,' I said, and it was true. At that moment I felt stronger and more alive than I had ever felt in my life.

'Will you still want me I wonder,' she said sadly, 'when you can have your choice of any woman on the mountain?'

'You silly goose! Of course I'll want you,' I laughed. 'What would be the point of my being here otherwise?'

She kissed my foot as she painted the nails, kissed the foot that was so twisted and deformed. The kiss felt like a blessing. Then I was ready to descend the stairs to the door into the bright sunshine.

The chanting and music drew me across the courtyard to take my place among the worshippers. From time to time people in the crowd would get up to dance, others called out in strange tongues; with each passing moment the air of religious rapture built higher.

When my name was called, my brain was so drunk that I felt I was no longer ugly and crippled. I was a giant! I could do anything! My feet took me to join in the dancing, whirling around the fire, feeling the heat from the hot coals burning my legs; and not caring.

Then I was walking in the procession, walking proud and straight - or so it seemed to me, walking without hesitation, feeling only a tingling of the skin where Alyssa had kissed and caressed my crippled foot, striding barefoot across the glowing red stones on the bed of burning logs, as the priest intoned the prayers and litanies peculiar to our religion.

At the end, the priest stood to inspect the soles of the feet of those who had walked the coals, and my father waited to greet me with my mother at his side.

'Jarvis, I never thought that I'd live to see this day,' father said as he embraced me. 'Now the ceremony is over whom will you choose as your bride?'

'Alyssa. I choose Alyssa,' I said.

The priest stopped and turned to where I was standing, 'Choose another! Alyssa has been given as a sacrifice to the Gods.'

Never before had I felt such fear and rage: Alyssa! My beautiful Alyssa condemned to be thrown in the flames like a lump of timber! That exquisite skin melting and burning! Her lovely hair withering on her head, those bottomless eyes filled with terror and pain... No! Never!

'Damn you, and damn your gods. Alyssa is mine,' I bellowed, 'She will be no sacrifice.'

Picking up a white-hot stone from the fire I flung it at the priest; it hit him on the arm.

'Your mother has donated her to the temple,' the priest roared, 'Would you steal from the gods?'

Were there no limits to the wounds my mother could inflict on me?

I picked up another stone, 'Damn you to Hell, Mother.'

As I took aim, Father grabbed me in a bear hug, 'Wait my son! Jarvis stop!'

He turned to the priest, 'I will buy the girl from the temple.'

'Only he who gave to the Gods, may take from the Gods,' said the priest.

'Then I will see that it is done.'

Mother walked towards us, 'Why would you do that?'

'Look at him wife! Look at your son! Are you so blind that you can't see what you have done?'

She stopped in front of me to stare into my eyes.

I lifted my head and stared back at her.

For a long moment we gazed at each other like enemies on a battlefield.

Then unexpectedly her eyes softened, as if she was seeing me for the first time.

A tiny trace of a smile; barely there.

A slight warmth; scarcely noticeable.

Turning to the priest she said; 'Old man, I will pay the bride price.'

And I dared to hope..."

'And was your hope fulfilled?' I asked.

'Judge for yourself,' he answered as a chariot drove into the courtyard.

The driver gestured at the wine, 'Hello my son. Don't drink it all. Save some for me!'

A young woman, a golden disc swinging on a heavy chain about her neck dismounted from behind him, and bent to kiss my host, and the older woman, who had been sitting beside her, smiled lovingly at the small boy standing between her knees; and turned her shining smile on Jarvis.

# Matthew Shelton-Jones

*I am employed in seeking creative outlets in music, cartoon doodlings and writing poetry and short stories (as well as writing music and cartoon stories), and I work in exam marking on the side. Also I identify storylines in dreams (as far as possible), in the form of writing 'dream diaries'.*

# A Hiker's Dream

Walking 'midst the blue and green,
Some may find it quite obscene
To worry about wearing socks
That seem to have on them a pox.
O'ernight I dreamt their holes are growing;
Later on that truth is showing.
Hole-y as they are, will they
Be meeting with their maker, pray?
Changing shoes is when I find
My socks leave earthly fears behind,
But will their worries wash away
All because we hiked today?
A gusty breeze; the bluebells stir.
Realities too often blur;
The sun shines on, and dreams come true,
Walking 'midst the green and blue.

# Niall Drennan

*I still haven't grown up - my children are much older than I am! I write and perform spoken word in various places. I'm also part of the PubCrawlPoets, a group of oldsters who will frequent any place where the spoken word is practiced and make our own, often inebriated, contribution. I have published various short stories and word pieces and I recorded words and music on the Factory label many moons ago.*

Niall Drennan

# Prince Amongst Princes


-Is one expected to eat this swill?
Prince Andrew was up to his old
tricks, attempting to impress a
young waitress he wanted to have
sex with in a Chelsea restaurant.
Unfortunately it was a waiter who
came over,
-You don't like?
-No I bloody don't but I'll have
some of this!
He sank his fork into the waiter's
arm and began to slice the man's
fingers off with his steak knife.
The digits dropped to his plate as
the waiter squealed and was led
away by the Maître De.
Crunching on a thumb served in a
Hollandaise sauce Andrew said,
-Can't bear background noise
when I'm eating!

# Fear

She was beautiful
to look at - all sleek
lines and feline grace.
His girlfriend purred
alongside her new
pet and both hissed
at him when he said,
-Why didn't you tell
me you were going to
get a cat?
-I don't have to tell
you everything!
-But I thought we
were going to live
together?
-And when we do...
she said,
-I'm bringing
her with me!
-But I don't want
you to...
-You would if you
loved me, she said
On hearing this he
blocked her number
on his phone and bought
a dog for protection.

# Coping

She coped.

Most of the time. Sometimes though she didn't. Cope.

This was one of those times. It was a bad day. A beastly day

She had coped. Up until now. Seven months and three days. Two months short of a full-term pregnancy.

One day at a time. That was what they said.

When she woke up it wasn't the drink. It was the being alone.

Worst was the bleak winter mornings when she heard susurrus voices all about her.

She needed to make more of an effort to help others.

Make contact with people.

She began with a letter.

*Dear Mr Sutcliffe,*

*I hope you don't mind me writing to you. My name is Sally and I am 39 (and still of a child bearing age as my mother likes to remind me). I live in London where besides my job as a librarian I enjoy reading, shopping and bird watching and - and this is where you come in - spending my free time helping other people.*

*I am writing to you with a view for us to become pen pals.*

*You are the first serial sex killer I have ever written to. However, I must stress I am not interested in the past. I want to become acquainted with the 'real' you, the present person. You see I feel that 'now' is the only real time we have. We must live in the present moment. There is no point brooding about life's tragedies.*

*I am sure that you, of all people can appreciate this.*

*I do look forward to hearing from you.*

*Yours*

**Sally Gallant**

She received an official letter back from Broadmoor Hospital four weeks later.

*Dear Madam,*

*I have discussed your recent letter with my patient. He informs me that he does not wish to enter into any correspondence with you. Please find your original letter enclosed.*

*Yours faithfully*

**Dr Phillip Norris**
**Consultant Forensic Psychiatrist**
**Clinical Director**
**Broadmoor SDU**

This was a setback. It was to be expected though. Faith was needed. In the afternoon, after she had been to church and listened to that beautiful sermon, she wrote another letter.

*Dear Mr Huntley,*

*I hope you don't mind me writing to you. My name is Sally and I am 39 (and still of a child bearing age as my mother likes to remind me). I live in London where besides my job as a librarian I enjoy reading, shopping and bird watching and - and this is where you come in - spending my free time helping other people.*

*I am writing to you with a view to us becoming pen pals.*

*You are the first child killer I have ever written to. However, I must stress I am not interested in the past. I want to become acquainted with the 'real' you, the present person. You see I feel that 'now' is the only real time we have. We must live in the present moment. There is no point brooding about life's tragedies.*

*I am sure that you of all people can appreciate this.*

*I do look forward to hearing from you.*

*Yours*

**Sally Gallant**

She received the official letter back from Wakefield Prison four weeks later.

*Dear Madam,*

*After a discussion about your letter with the intended prisoner, I regret to inform you no further correspondence will be entered into. Find your original letter enclosed.*

*Yours faithfully,*

**Susan Howard**
**Governor**
**HMP Wakefield**
**5 Love Lane**
**Wakefield**
**West Yorkshire**
**WF2 9AG**

She was disappointed and wondered if the bitch had even let him see the letter. Never mind.

The idea for the next letter hit her when she was on her way back with the shopping.

Later that evening with her Parker Vector fountain pen and a cup of tea by her side she began to write:

*My Condolences,*

*First off I would like to offer my deepest sympathy for your loss. I hope you don't mind me writing to you. My name is Sally and I am 39 (and still of a child bearing age as my mother likes to remind me). I live in London where besides my job as a librarian I enjoy reading, shopping and bird watching and - and this is where you come in - spending my free time helping other people.*

*I am writing to you with a view to us becoming pen pals.*

*I understand that as a mother your life must have been turned upside down following your daughter's death.*

*I have so many questions to ask. Have you had another child? Are you religious? What do you do with your time?*

*This is the first time I have written to the mother of a murdered child.*

*However, I must stress I am not interested in the past. I want to become acquainted with the 'real' you, the present person. You see I feel that 'now' is our only real time. We must live in the present moment. There is no point brooding about life's tragedies.*

*I am sure that you of all people can appreciate this.*

*I do look forward to hearing from you.*

*Yours*

**Sally Gallant**

*PS.  I am sure that to have coped with such trauma in your life, you too, like me, must be a deeply spiritual person.*

Even before she posted the letter, her mood had begun to improve.

## Niall Drennan

## Lover

I was careless at the party
Smoking and drinking next to our house
The blaze could be seen for miles.
In the aftermath my lover vanished
Everyone knew I was responsible.
For three weeks I was inconsolable with grief
Then I found a new lover. We slept in the car on the ashes of the
fire.
We were immersed in passionate lovemaking when the wailing
began.
It came from a flowerbed.
I was surprised to see my old lover rise from the soil.
A diet of insects, rainwater and a love for me had made survival
possible.
We celebrated this miracle by pouring three glasses of wine
and sat down to consider the situation
In the end I decided that I preferred my newfound love
on account the fire had made my old lover wizened
and charred with crinkly, black skin.

# Noreen Brown

*I have been a social worker and dairy farmer in New Zealand and Australia, and published my first novel 'Shadows Before' in 2011, through Brighton NightWriters press*

## .Black Swans

Till I was fourteen I didn't question my Catholic upbringing. Then one day I heard Mam argue with Grandma. They often had arguments. Grandma was shouting. "If you'd listened to me, your life would have been different. And another thing - you haven't been to confession for months. How do you expect God to forgive you?" I moved closer to the door. "God" my mother shouted. I'd never heard her shout like that before. "Don't talk to me about God. Where was he when Wyn took off and left us? Me with three under four. Where was he when Noreen was born in a workhouse? Don't talk to me about God."

From that day, I found myself watching and listening for sights and sounds of God helping people. But all I saw was people praying, getting drunk and beating up the mothers of their kids. And kids without any shoes and going to school with no lunch. "Me Mam can't afford the bread," Michael said when I asked. "And me Dad's in prison and me uncles are working in England." I gave him a bit of my sandwich. He wiped his nose on his sleeve and grinned. "Sometimes they send us money but we have to give it to Mam and never tell Dad." I tried to talk to Nuala my best friend and Maureen, but they said I'd go to hell if I didn't believe in God. I never found anyone who felt like me.

And then I was sent on a retreat which was scary and wonderful and made me want to believe again, but that's another story.

Soon after that, we went to England. We got the night train to Holyhead and shuffled along the gang plank with mostly lots of young people all excited. Seeking their fortunes, Mam said. It was freezing and I was glad of my new green heavy coat with a huge button at the neck that Mam bought on the never. Just before we left. We only paid for half of it but Grandma said as we were so poor God would forgive us.

On the ship, before I became seasick, I heard two women talking and laughing and one said, "Sure I haven't been to confession for years. Me sins are so bad God would never forgive me." They both laughed and laughed and nudged each other. I wanted to talk to them but Grandma was watching me so I pretended not to be listening and then the dark one said, "It's a terrible thing but I have me doubts about God." My ears pricked up and I so wished to talk to them but

Grandma said, "Come on child. Let's move away from these heathen women."

But the seed had been sown. And a few years after living in Clapham a priest called and asked to speak to me. I'd been to confession twice but I never knew how he found me. He was a really kind man and he spoke in a soft voice and I wished I wasn't different to everyone else. But in London it wasn't like Dublin. Lots of nice people didn't go to mass.

We argued on the doorstep and his last words were "And what about your immortal soul?"

So for a few months I started going to mass but eventually my visits dwindled and Grandma gave up on me. Mam never told me off. She didn't try to persuade me but I knew ever since we left Ireland. She'd really lost the faith.

Many many years later, when I was much older, I went on a writing holiday which was held in an annexe in the grounds of an ancient monastery. It was an unforgettable, dreamlike experience.

One morning, on impulse, I entered the small church attached to the monastery. Candle flames soared and flickered at each end of the altar.

The worn pews stood in silent witness. Memories flooded. I am seventeen again, it is my last confession before committing the unforgivable. Having sex and not married.

As I stare unseeing at the old familiar, the graphic depiction of Jesus on the cross, there is a movement by my side. I turn to the robed figure.

"Are you of the faith?" he asks mildly.

I look into his tired, seen-it-all eyes.

"No! I'm not. I'm not of any faith," I say, immediately regretting my dismissive reply.

He nods, non-committal, then by unspoken consent we turn from the altar and walk side by side down the long aisle. Sunlight streams through the figured windows. Dust motes dance at our feet.

Outside we step carefully over crunching stones, keeping our distance.

Staring straight ahead, his flowing dark robes whispering, billowing, his voice low he says, "Do you miss the faith?"

Startled, I look at him. He stops, faces me.

"My child, you don't have to say. I watched you enter. Saw how you knelt, how you bowed your head."

He touches my arm. Incense wafts. I look down at his slim wrinkled hand. At the ring, glinting on his finger.

"If you have known the faith it is embedded. Watchful and silent it waits. Ready to comfort, to support, to console in your hour of need."

I wrestle with denial. Ridicule. Irony. Decide not. This is a moment to cherish. SMILE.

We are walking towards the lake now. A willow tree weeps the surface smooth.

If only I could go back to those early years. Unquestioning belief. The comfort of knowing God would protect me. Forgive me for my sins.

If only. Tears blur as I gaze ahead.

Two black swans, their necks entwined, float motionless, the devils on my shoulder.

He sighs gently. He puts a small crucifix to his mouth, kisses it lightly, says, "Go in peace my child. And safe journey home."

The swans swish across the sky, shadow the sunset.

As I walk, head bent, a bell intones the hour.

# Oliver Andrew

*Now retired, I spend summers
in France recycling myself as a
French peasant, and winters in
Brighton keeping warm
(I know that may seem
paradoxical).
I write poetry, and articles on
such things as philately, travel
etc, and have recently
completed a novel.*

Oliver Andrew

# Off the Azores

We're no longer alone:
We're crossing a motorway
In sea-mist, on a sleek swell,
Engine and Portuguese stop,
Open-mouthed the sailors listen
About to remember something.

There, yards away, a black iceberg
      up...
Rolls      over ...
                  long ....
     longer ...
And more everywhere as big as museums
Echo the first, shapeless as swollen lights,
Huge hushing snorting pops -
Temporary islands are breathing all around.

Next to the boat
A calf the size of your kitchen slides over,
Blows oily, fishy, salty
Memories of our waterlogged womb -
Can we be friends?

A tail rises, a clutch of barnacles on the left fluke,
They're going down, one after the other,
Blank sea-sheep, just warm fish,
These meteors of blubber plunge out of our lives,
Return us to the mist
Now sprayed with a fading stink,
In the present, laughing and cheering,
We're on our own.

# Couples

In every couple, there's one to fret
And one to sleep
There's one to find the world a threat
And one to weep
One a self-dramatizer
One a self-justifier
One who confides and one who doubts
One who sings and one who shouts

But when is who which?

Oliver Andrew

# It's an obstacle race

A brimming glass of water
Is given to you
And you're off:
Some dribbles, some slops -
They're yours too.

Some put a hand over,
Seal it off forever;
Sniggering, away they go:
      Er........ no.

 Myra gives hers to Ian.
Like his own he chucks most away
For the hell of it.
She claims it back, calling:
"Look, I didn't spill a drop."

# Nature Poem

A stiff head on the blackthorn.
Blades of daffodil and iris
Stubble the mud. A pettish rain
Has camped on the doorstep.
Branches spar with the wind.

In summer, a breezeless heat
Lies torpid as a sea of treacle.
Shape rocks a feather to earth.
Flax is a shimmering sloping lake.
 At night the stars are restive,
An unwearied moon comforts them.

Down with green!
When autumn bares a gull-yellow eye
Opposition chars.

And winter's clear minimum
Is not what it seems -
Trees whose fat fruit is pigeons,
An empty chair.

But sharp or stilled or absent,
That's the world of words,
Where everything's like some other thing.
A rising steam, a ghostly breath of wit
No deer can sense;
But they, like rocks and trees,
Don't even shrug;
It's things that are themselves
Indifferently -
Light, chance, time -
That swaddle, ripen, bleach and perish
That change them.

Oliver Andrew

# Solvitur ambulando

I'm a pack of clueless tensions. But motion's no problem:
Walking takes me out through the suburbs,
                                        past black privet hedges,
By private, steaming fences, along the hidden verges -
Already some signs: "Keep off the Grass", "Diversion,"
                                        - adorn them,

On thin snow that nobody's trodden since snow first began.
I trample its monotone fragility, now melting
To uncover warm toughness, as the Earth, slowly tilting,
Slackens the cold-tangled knots, announces its colour-plan.

Ice and sunlight abandon their grey glitter below
The dripping, basic trees. Gardens grow browner and darker.
There are footprints, meaning others have passed here. I walk a
Slippery mud tightrope unravelling across the snow
What's white now will soon be green, yellow, rose.
                                        I reach my marker,
Then turn home, all the way becoming clearer to know.

# Patrick Evans

*I'm a Canadian writer and journalist who recently moved to Brighton to have my mid-life crisis on the beach. My fiction has recently been published in* Strangely Funny II *and* Krampusnacht: Twelve Nights of Krampus.

# Hump Song

Every night I turned off the electrical currents crackling in my castle laboratory and traded my lab coat for a tuxedo. I sat in my box at the opera house and worshipped her down there on the stage, worshipped the sublime beauty of her face, her form, and above all, her voice - a voice that would make a choir of angels throw down their harps in an envious rage.

*"Vissi d'arte, vissi d'amore,"* she sang. She lived for art, she lived for love. Like me! As artists we were preeminent in our fields. Her voice had made her the toast of Europe. My inventions, which tended to run amok, cutting swathes of destruction across the continent, had made me the toast of mad scientists. We had so much in common, she and I.

I could no longer bear just watching her from a distance. She had to be mine. I summoned Igor, my hunchbacked lab assistant, and ordered him to seize her, to bring her to my castle.

Igor covered himself with lard so his hump might better slide down the chimney into her dressing room. The abduction went perfectly. But when that fool was carrying my beloved over the castle drawbridge he was so greasy she squeaked out of his arms like a wet bar of soap. She fell into the moat where her magnificent body was ravaged by a pair of giant carnivorous goldfish I had created with a diet of secret elixir and pork tenderloin.

And yet there remained a spark of life in her! Her body was ruined, but if I acted fast enough I might still preserve her sublime voice. I carried her down the winding stone steps to my laboratory. I needed living tissue for a transplant. In desperation I placed her brain, mouth, and vocal cords into Igor's hump.

I bade the hump to sing - and the voice was perfection.

*"Vissi d'arte, vissi d'amore...."*

But there was a problem. Igor was accompanying her.

*"Vishy darty! Vishy dumry! Ha-HO!"*

I told him to shut up. He wouldn't. He couldn't! Tests revealed the problem was organic. Their nervous systems had merged. When she sang, he sang too.

In disgust I banished them to the scullery. But the castle walls are thin and every day I hear their cacophonous duet.

It is unbearable. I would have thrown myself from the castle turret months ago were it not for the student intern who replaced Igor in the lab. She can't carry a tune, but those long legs and short skirts of hers are slowly restoring my tormented soul.

# PHAEDON

*My goal is to transport you to worlds of imagination, invention and adventure, enriching your life with vibrancy, emotion and treasured moments. It all started with an award-winning short story.*
*Keep in touch with me via*
phaedon.me *and* fayjayworld.com

# 40 minutes

The alarm goes off
on my mobile phone
calming, soothing, Air on the G string;
I tense up immediately.
I was waiting for it.
 -40.
Awake or asleep, I'm always
waiting for it.
Activate all systems,
get the synapses firing,
hit the shower
till -25.
I'm already clean, but I need
my body to understand,
to calm my feelings down
to null.
I moisturise then,
it's a damaging environment
I'm preparing to step in
for the skin, especially.
Next, I proceed to put on
the prothoraxic shirt and tie, in the company colours of course,
followed by the arthropod trousers
and shoes in black.
Then I wax my hair back,
smooth as an epicranium,
and I slip on the pterothoraxic waistcoat
with my name tagged, bull's-eye, over the heart.
The wings fit on top of that
in the shape of a metal brooch, pinned on a jacket, black.

# Night Flights

At -5 I survey the insect drone
in the mirror looking back.
It is impressively ready for honeyless service –
servitude – with its insect hands sorting things out
with its insect feet balancing on the flying metal grid
of the alien-airline, mother ship.
And the forty minutes are up.
Time to go, time to make
a lifeless living. No more atomic thoughts
and no more atomic feelings.
I wish the self-loathing
would not kick in, four flights onward,
as I return home
with that wobbly feeling in my brain,
with my feet still thinking they're on the plane,
with my organs inflated, deflated and dry,
with my brain sick by the hive's drone
and my flesh asphyxiating in the company-issued exoskeleton.
So little was gained from yet another day:
"I was not myself today,
I was not myself
today."

# Dool

The Kisskimoe cub was cleaning the arms hearth. The Great Grand Myster insisted on it. Great, grand things were expected of her. She would be a fully flared *Clan Flame* soon and she needed to acquire *The Gift of the Hearth,* as it was known. That meant she was to slave and train to within an inch of her sanity until she became War Master and Protector of Swords.

*War Master and Protector of Swords...*

The words sounded harsh and heavy to her. Just like her responsibilities. Alone, as required, she worked her claws to stubs scrubbing the hearth with a wire brush and mordant sap, her fur becoming knotted and filthy as a result. Not that it made a huge difference. From lumpy black, the Womb of the Fireswords became only the slightest bit smoother. It would never be truly clean, though, scrub as she may.

*Great, grand things indeed...*

She pursed her lips and put more elbow into it, panting with exertion, her aspirations flashing before her eyes, the frustration growing with every impossible attempt. She expected grander and greater things for herself – beyond the visions of the Ministry of Mysters. She wanted to climb the Atta Mountain and look at what lay beyond. She wanted to sail through the Frozen Waters and burrow through the Barren Caves, places the Kisskimoes only whispered about in fear. She wanted to find out what was *really* out there.

"Poppyscotch!" the Mysters scolded. "There's nothing but the Great White Emptiness out there. Nothing but the Great White Emptiness and the Black Terrors."

They never did offer an adequate explanation as to what either of those things were, exactly. They offered tales about shady creatures creeping along the borders of Kisskim, mouths full of pointy teeth, claws poised to catch ambitious cubs straying out into the unknown beyond. What exactly happened to the cubs once they got caught was, also, left to the imagination. But she was not a cub anymore! Well not a *cub* cub ... The grubby soot gushing endlessly out of the hearth, engulfing her bit by bit, was the true Black Terror, as far as she was concerned.

"Ah!" she cried in despair as she tried to reach deeper and fell face first into the soot, arms outstretched in front of her.

*Clink!*

It didn't sound like metal. She flicked her claws again into the darkness overhead.

*Clink!* The thing repeated. She shuffled further in and began to fumble around. *What in the world could remain solid, buried so deep in the core of the hearth? Its blaze turned minerals to liquids and everything else to cinders and smoke!* It was beginning to feel like a large globe. Sturdy. Glassy. Containing some sort of liquid. *An unfired fireball?* That would be extremely dangerous, she knew. But no enemy had ever edged this deep into the heart of Kisskim. *This is surely something else.* She crawled out, dragging the object under the candlelight. It was almost completely covered in grime, yet she discerned a certain *sparkling* under it. She twisted round and wiped it with her back fur, which was somewhat cleaner than the rest of her.

"A Giant's Eyeball!" she marvelled when she gazed back at it. She blinked. The orb was glowing opalescent and semi-translucent. A pure, warm, sunset light seemed to emanate from within it. The Giants of the Sun perished infinite winters ago, she knew. The myths were never clear as to why. But glimmering globes like this one were said to have been discovered through the ages, rare remnants of those bygone beings. They were supposed to preserve within them the last sight beheld by the Giants at the moment of their death and bestow gargantuan wisdom and power to the brave Kisskimoe who could look into their depths and see with a Giant's eye.

*To see with a Giant's eye...*

"Great goodness, I'll be the greatest, grandest Kisskimoe that has ever lived!" she screeched happily.

The orb slipped through her hands smashing horribly onto the sooty stone floor. She shrieked as the hearth room shook and erupted into blinding light. Then softness enveloped her, softness, as she had never felt. A cloudy, glittering softness. Rainbows shot out of it and disappeared. Pink, horned and winged beings trotted around in it, around her. They all seemed so happy. She felt strangely joyful to be in their midst. She couldn't help it. She was quite shocked at first, but it didn't last long. She jumped and pranced around in the twirling universe. She was floating, all movement delightfully slow and light. Pearly particles twinkled all around. The creatures of happiness were dancing in space and she felt perfectly giddy watching their swirling acrobatics. Jumping up herself, she caught one by its long, graceful neck. It was the prettiest creature she had ever met. It turned around and smiled at her, eyes brimming with kindness. She nuzzled at its vast pink nose.

"Dool," it said sweetly.

And vanished.

"Dool?" she asked before she knew that all the joy was gone, searing pain shooting up from her limbs, making her scream.

She found herself kneeling among the shards of the orb, bleeding from her hands and knees. She sobbed in despair, uncomprehending, more alone and tired and hurt than she had ever felt before, on the cold, hard, sooty floor, the hearth room empty, full of swords, just as it was before.

# Rags and Stuffing

They slept with Mr Snuggles every night. Inert and inanimate as they were, they ... began to feel something ... in the long run. It was inevitable really. When you spend so many hours daily – or nightly as in their case – with someone, you are bound to start developing some sort of bond with them, aren't you? And they usually spent six or seven of the 24 hours cuddling with Mr Snuggles. That's all he had time for, being very busy creating wonderful gifts for all the creatures of the universe in his shop.

They were gifts given to him from another creature, who loved Mr Snuggles very much, but had to be away. It didn't matter to them at all, initially, though things did change over time. The gawky one, Mr Snuggles called Zoops. It was black and white, with a squishy, round belly and four long, floppy limbs dangling from its edges, as well as a little, floppy tail with a black tuft at the end. The other one was pink and squat, with a pearly horn on the tip of its muzzle, iridescent wings on its back and silver stars on its hindquarters. It had a long, fluffy, white tail and was named Engelbert.

Mr Snuggles pressed them to his chest after turning the lights off and they felt his heartbeat. Beat ... beat ... beat ... He grew very attached to them. When he switched sides in his sleep, he always carried them with him, to the other side. They swayed up and down along the rhythm of his breathing. Even though they did not have lungs themselves, they began to resonate with something like life in the quiet of the night. And even without a heart of their own, their bodies beat to the sound of his.

Beat, beat, beat, beat ... something was wrong with him ... Suddenly Mr Snuggles began to spend longer hours sleeping, yet not resting. He tossed and turned and rolled them endlessly around with him. He clenched them to his chest, so close, they would have gasped and protested had they been truly alive. They did not have working eyes, or functioning ears, but they suffered his distress, got drenched in his sweat and even tasted his tears. They had to do something. And though they had no bones, no muscles and nothing but stuffing in their head they concentrated. Hard.

Beat ... beat ... beat, beat, beat, beat ... they finally managed to reach the other side of sleep. Their eyes blinking open, more than decorative, saw *The Blight*, as they would come to call it – a vicious thing, much denser than the night. It squeezed Mr Snuggles within the folds of its massive, scaly tail, enveloping his tiny frame in bone-crunching sinew. Its scabby hands clutched him by the throat, the claws digging into his sallow flesh. His eyes bulged, wide open, yet unseeing, his tongue hung from his mouth, the thing gulping down his living breath, gouging it out of his lungs with its dry and leathery tongue, hissing awful things inside his ear.

"Give me your life. Surrender it to me. Your love has gone away and left you. You have nothing. You have no one."

They kicked and neighed in horror. Startled, *The Blight* scowled at them through sad and desperate eyes. And it began to laugh.

"What are you going to do about it?" it screeched. "You are nothing but rags and stuffing!"

They charged. Zoops cobbled the thing with hooves whose softness seemed to burn holes into its substance. Engelbert flew up into the air and slashed at it with his sparkling horn. *The Blight* flinched and shrieked as the real night began to show through it, but it could not find a way to grasp or harm them without singeing gaps into itself, soft as they were all over.

"He is mine!" it spat as it finally released Mr Snuggles, and slithered away into the murkiest sliver of darkness it could find – so many holes in it, it looked almost transparent. "I will always come back for him! I will always find a way!"

Engelbert and Zoops did not know what a corpse looked like but there was an emptiness to Mr Snuggles they did not recognise. He seemed to be nothing but rags and stuffing himself.

"Mr Snuggles?" they begged and in that moment knew what love and life was, indeed. Zoops threw his gangling front limbs around his head in tears, attempting to nuzzle him back to them. Stubby, little Englebert tried to follow suit, but ended up poking Mr Snuggles's side with his horn.

"Ah!" gasped Mr Snuggles and he drew breath.

Zoops and Engelbert jumped for joy and snuggled sweetly up to him. They decided, then, that a bit of air might do him good, so

Zoops lifted Mr Snuggles onto Engelbert's back and the two of them flew out of the window. Zoops jumped out after them and galloped wildly, yipping away as they swooshed and cartwheeled above. The three of them saw, in their words, *All the wonderful gifts of the universe that night.* They felt all the pleasure and all the pain in the world. They saw all the baleful things that tortured other creatures and all the unexpected things that helped the creatures fight.

In the morning, Engelbert gave Mr Snuggles another tiny poke in his side to make sure he woke up. Mr Snuggles blinked his eyes open and gazed at the soft toys in his arms. They beamed back at him inert and inanimate as ever. He checked his heartbeat for some, unknown, reason. Beat. Beat. Beat. Beat. Exhausted though he was, after another restless night, he climbed out of the bed and kept busy all day in his shop, pressing himself to move again onwards, *Towards all the wonderful gifts of the universe,* he thought, unknowingly, smiling to himself. At night there was a rap at the door. The creature who loved him very much had come back.

# Rosemary Allix

*I have been hanging out with the
Brighton NightWriters for many
years, only taking time off to study
creative writing at Sussex
University (now an MA!).
I write anything, poetry, prose,
shopping lists ...
Find more of my writing on my website
https://rosemaryswebofwords.wordpress.com*

Rosemary Allix

# Gull In Winter

Late January.
An afternoon of
mildness
and wide bright sky.

He swoops
exploring
drifting in wide circles
on rising air.

Stands
motionless on the roof ridge
experiencing
analysing.

Squats
among a cluster of chimney pots
sheltered
but not yet content.

Launches
still searching
restless and aroused
by a promise of Spring.

Tomorrow.
Storms ground him
strong beak ripping plastic
on gum stained pavements.

# Morning Kitten

Dawn hinting
with a shift of air
one note of birdsong.
Uncurl, roll over, eyes open,
Tail switch, whiskers twitch.
Burrow deeper, darker
into soft rustling clouds and find
A foot,
familiar, no fur
irresistible.
Sniff, grab, nip.
Foot vanishes
But only a chase away wrapped up
waiting to be explored, discovered, gnawed.

First light creeping behind the curtains.
Stalking an arm,
a hand
fingers.
At last attention
More, more, more
delightful tickling stroking.
Rolling
Curling
Rumbling throat

Full day, sunshine, action.
Stirring
Emerging.
Run downstairs to get there first.
Alarm!
Bowl's empty
But not for long.
Satisfying
Energising
Race for the door
Leap
bound, scamper
in the dampness of dew.

# At the Crowded Bus Stop

A couple
Not young
Absorbed in each other
And their two miniature dogs.

He leans in
Picks a peeling flake off her sunburnt shoulder.
An intimate gesture
Revealing long familiarity
With her skin,
Her bones, her flesh.
Compliant to his familiar grooming
She murmurs words
Strokes the ears
Of the tiny dog in her arms.

Their bus arrives.
He picks up his dog
Speaks to him like a son
Explains
'Time to go home'.
Their bubble of togetherness drifts away
Leaving me lightly smudged
As I continue to wait alone
In my own small world
Where my bones are private
And nobody knows the qualities of my skin.

Rosemary Allix

# Cinderella – After the Ball

Briefly I danced in your world,
my happiness fat as a pumpkin,
all the rats and toads transformed.
In the hour before midnight I was beautiful,
admired, desired, in the hour
before the clock struck twelve.

What story do you tell yourself now?
What tale of once upon a time?
Do I still glide in your arms?
Does my perfume cling? Do you remember
warm jewels and whispering silk?
Was the illusion so well crafted it transformed me
into everything you wanted me to be?

You and I, we tasted magic. But have you guessed?
Have you worked it out? It was just fantasy,
a mirage,  a one-night-only conjuring trick.
In the morning you walk out secure and proud
while I hide from the light in my poverty and shame.
There is no rainbow bridge between your world and mine.

Hold tight to my ragged shoe. A poor thing,
but in your eyes a slipper of glass,
a talisman, a memory of our one perfect dance.
You believe in a vanished princess, but your faith
is the only thing keeping the magic alive.
I know there is nobody to find but a kitchen maid.

I could not let you discover me now
in my habitat of rags and rats.
How ashamed I am of the real me
in my world of cinders and ash.
Look at me sweeping the floor, dreaming of my prince,
long after the spell is broken.

## Clouds

Among clouds lies illusion.

A great white tortoise,
Shape shifting into a forest,
Slipping behind a grey veil.

Pushed by winds
Obedient to pressure zones raised by mountain peaks
Or the flutter of a butterfly wing.

Among the soft pillows of giants, a tiny shiny arrowhead
A glint, a wink, before it vanishes,
Leaving its sky-long signature of fragile droplets.

Black, grey, silver in a sky of bluebell, turquoise,
Continually transformed by the refraction of split-up sunshine.
And the sea colludes.

Watch the  passing sky
And recognise illusion.

# The Transformation of Martha

Martha was preparing a steak and kidney pudding. Onions sliced and fried, meat chopped into cubes, browned to seal in the juices, stir in a rich gravy and seal it all inside a comforting slab of suet pastry. A large pot of water was coming to the boil, she stretched her ample body over the hob to check  progress and steam rose up into her face. Something dripped into the pan. Another something followed, drip, drop. Martha saw what looked like globules of white fat jumping and twisting in the bubbling water.

She watched fascinated. Where were these fat balls coming from? She passed a hand over her hot steamy face and a torrent of liquid lard plopped down into the pan. Martha drew back alarmed and caught sight of a face reflected in the glass door of a kitchen cupboard. A stranger stared back. A woman with a strong lean face and prominent cheek bones.

She rushed upstairs and studied herself properly in the bedroom mirror. Her plain plump face was transformed. Quickly she picked up her hairbrush, pulled off the band holding back her dark lank hair and started to brush vigorously forward to cover the shocking unfamiliarity of her face. With each stroke of the brush her hair grew paler, blonder, streaks of sunshine amid the darkness, tresses of hair swelling, filling in volume, kinking and curling around the new firm chin, over the smooth alabaster brow.

Martha no longer recognised herself. She did however recognise the face in the mirror, it was the face of a well known television star and model, a woman considered a great beauty, she couldn't think of her name but she had seen her enough times on the screen to realise that she now seemed to have this woman's head.

Shocked she stepped back and gazed at herself. The glamorous head looked ridiculous on Martha's fat body, the tightly boned face perched above rolls of flesh crammed into a Lycra top, spilling over straining jogging bottoms. She backed slowly out of the bedroom away from the frightening mirror but still watching her reflection. On the landing her foot caught in a tear in the frayed carpet and unable to grab anything to save herself she began to fall.

She fell down the stairs. Not painfully or unkindly, but with a floating fall like a balloon. Each time her body bounced off a stair, off the banisters, off the window sill half way down, it shed a part of itself. Balls of discarded Martha settled on the treads like uncooked steak and kidney puddings. By the time she landed, with a breath snatching jolt, on the tiles of the front hall she was a perfect size ten. Slowly she picked herself up and smoothed her baggy clothes against her new shape.

Just then the front door crashed open. "Hi, Mum." He two sons rushed past her into the kitchen, she heard the thud of dropped football boots, the rattle of the biscuit tin, the crash of the back door flung open.

Her teenage daughter sauntered in, eyes fixed on the screen of her phone.

"Hello." Martha whispered.

"Hi." And she was gone, up the stairs, weaving an unseeing path between the fat balls.

When Martha's husband came home he too didn't seem to notice the transformation of his wife from dumpy housefrau to glamorous supermodel. He did notice, however, that his dinner was late and when it arrived in front of him it was nothing more substantial than an unsatisfactory salad.

Next day Martha went shopping. She called in at the bank and emptied the children's savings accounts, then she hit the boutiques where assistants perked up and rushed forward at the sight of her, offering fashion advice, praising her taste, her figure, her elegance.

With four carrier bags in one hand, stiff white shiny ones with string handles, and a new lime green leather handbag in the other, she headed for the station, stopping off only once at a shop selling all sizes of suitcases. Heads turned as she passed by. At the station she consulted timetables for trains to Heathrow, boarded the next appropriate one, arrived at the airport and checked in her new luggage on a flight to Hollywood.

Sitting in the departure lounge she began to think about her family. Would they miss her? Would they notice she had gone? Would they remember to feed the cat? A slight worry started to niggle at her mind. How would it be if she never saw any of them again, never again stood on a cold wet football field cheering on her boys, never again leaned against a closed door on the landing attempting conversation with her hysterical daughter. Would her husband marry again? Would someone else stand at her kitchen stove, chopping onions, rolling out suet crust pastry.

A woman sat down heavily in the seat next to her, she was plain, tubby and poorly dressed, she sighed as her body collapsed onto the cold plastic chair. Martha crossed one long elegant leg over the other and briefly felt a smug satisfaction as she compared her legs to the solid tree trunks of her neighbour.

Then her body began to slip sideways, as if magnetised she felt herself being sucked in towards the fat woman, felt her brittle elegance being absorbed into the other's comforting solidity as she was swallowed up, drowning in flesh and fat.

Martha stood up, shook herself slowly, picked up her Tesco carrier bag and began to plod slowly home.

# Sharon Board

*I have lived in Brighton for 13 years after moving from London with my three children. I studied English language and literature with the Open University and have attended various writing courses. Since joining the NightWriters group I have become interested in writing short crime stories.*

# Unknown Number

'What the hell' groaned Kate as she reached for her phone. The drum sound seemed a good idea at the time of setting her new ring tone, now at 4am on Sunday, it was extremely irritating. As Kate stared at the unknown number, she was unsure whether to answer, but having been woken up she answered abruptly 'Who is this?'

'Sorry Ma'am, to disturb you at this time but a body has been found and er...'

'Who is this and why is this number blocked,' shouted Kate.

'Sorry ma'am, this is DI Saunders and I'm new to the investigation, I have just been brought in to help..'

Kate interrupted as she was now getting impatient,

'What, why the hell am I not told about new team members, oh never mind, ok I will be right there, which is where exactly?' Kate snapped.

As Kate hurried to get ready, she really wished she hadn't drunk the whole bottle of red last night and she massaged her head hoping for some instant relief.

'Shit,' Kate cursed as she dropped her phone, the cover came off and the battery went crashing onto the floor. Kate grabbed the pieces and threw them into her bag, she wouldn't need the phone yet, she knew where to go. 'Bloody Ditchling Beacon, what is it with dog walkers during the night finding bodies? Well if it means we catch this bastard then good for them reporting it' Kate angrily said to herself.

Kate was still amazed how much traffic there was at 4.30 am. 'Don't people go to sleep in this town' she said aloud as she increased her speed along Ditchling Road. 'God I wish they would let me know when new people are brought into an investigation and why wasn't DI Scott Meadows, dealing with this?'

Kate was still feeling light-headed after the wine and lack of sleep; this was the last thing she wanted at this time.

Kate sighed as she checked her reflection in the mirror, her normally neat brown bob was sticking up and she hadn't time to apply any make-up. Kate still looked younger than her 41 years and her small, slim frame, added to her youthful look. She turned up the volume as Mariah Carey sang *'We belong together'* and thought about Mark. Kate had only been going out with Mark for six months but she really felt they could have a future together. Kate loved the way Mark was so ambitious and had loads of positive energy about him; he was so easy to get on with and they got on so well. Mark had joined her team about a year ago and it was at the Christmas party that they finally got together, much to everyone's teasing as he was ten years her junior. Kate smiled as she thought about their night together last week and suddenly became excited about wanting to see Mark again very soon.

As the haggard looking man stared down at the blood stained naked body, he had a sickly smile as he looked around, waiting for Kate's appearance. 'She will be here any minute' he mumbled out loud. 'You two deserve each other' he said aloud and laughed deeply. 'Your dear Kate will soon be joining you.'

When Scott Meadows joined the police force in Brighton he became instant friends with Derek, a promising, detective. Derek took Scott under his wing and encouraged him to think outside of the box when dealing with situations. They were very similar in their looks and were often mistaken for brothers. Both had short, fair hair and were of similar medium build. Derek introduced Scott to the local gym and they both worked out when they had time off together. Derek told Scott about how he had fallen in love with a remarkable woman, except she didn't know about it yet, and that he was planning to propose. They both laughed at his statement and Scott teased him no end about the whole unlikely event. Derek insisted she was the one and that one day Scott would be a witness to their mutual vows.

During their rare nights off, Scott would supply the beers and Derek the food, which was generally a Chinese. When Scott heard about a promotion, he started to spend more time at work, trying to impress Kate.

Derek became jealous of Scott's commitment to work and their relationship grew distant. Their friendship suffered and even though

Scott suggested they should still meet up Derek always had some excuse to decline the offer. Scott gave up trying and was surprised when Derek announced that he was transferring to another team in Worthing.

Scott hadn't heard from Derek for about two months and assumed he was getting on with his life. So it was a surprise for Scott to hear from Derek and to be invited to his new place in Brighton. Derek said he had been working undercover on a drugs deal and wanted Scott's opinion on the matter. Scott felt flattered and being ambitious he thought if he could get some credit in this operation then why not see what Derek was up to.

It was Saturday night and Derek smiled to himself as his plan was now beginning to form into reality. He gulped down his glass of Jameson and lit another cigarette, the overflowing ashtray and half bottle of whiskey was amongst a pile of screwed up photos. His normally neat blonde hair was long, dark and unwashed. Stubble covered Derek's face and his grubby clothes were hanging loose as he hadn't been eating well. He was on leave from work having been told he needed to take some time off. 'What do they know about emotional distress, stupid counsellors,' though he had to follow orders. 'Well I am bloody giving the orders now.'

Derek checked his watch, it was nearly 9pm and Scott would be here any minute, he smiled as he held up the sharpened knife.

Kate was near Ditchling Beacon and her car skidded at the bend that led to the car park. It was deserted except for a dirty white van. This is strange, Kate thought, where is everyone? She started to put her phone together to phone her colleagues, plus she wanted to text Mark to tell him she would drop by soon and give him an early wake up treat.

Kate couldn't get any reception. 'Shit, bloody countryside,' she cursed. Kate got out and walked further down the hill, it was then she noticed the figure of a man, looking at something in the ground.

Scott thought he would walk along the sea front to Derek's place as it was a nice evening and for a Saturday night it was fairly quiet.

Scott arrived on time and as he rang the bell he checked that he had enough beers. He was quite excited about seeing Derek again, he had missed their friendship and hoped they would be mates again.

'Hey Derek,' Scott greeted him and then stopped in mid sentence when he noticed the state Derek was in.

'Scott matey, come on in, let's get you a drink' Derek slurred. Scott was horrified to see the state of Derek and suppressed the need to retch as the stench of Derek's body odour blended with something else, something very unpleasant.

Scott reluctantly accepted a whiskey from a dirty glass out of politeness though he felt uneasy and felt himself start to sweat from anxiety. 'Come on Scotty, my loyal friend, drink up' Derek said as he clunked their glasses.

'Look Derek, what's going on, I thought you were ok and... arrh...' suddenly Scott felt a pain on his head and warm liquid covering his face. 'You bastard, treating me like shit; you think you can get away with this' Derek shouted. Scott was on the floor, feeling dazed and he could only just make out Derek's thin shape coming close to him, holding a knife and broken bottle, 'Hang on mate, what's going on', Scott said softly.

'Shut up, Derek interrupted, You have no right to talk and you are not my mate, do you hear me, no right and you're not my mate' Derek held the knife close to Scott's throat as he told him how he had betrayed their friendship for a stupid promotion.

'What, you've attacked me for that? Come on Derek, don't do anything stupid.'

Scott was struggling for breath and pleading, he was aware of the blood that was covering his face and dripping in his mouth.

Derek smiled as he held the sharpened knife close to Scott's soft skin and applied enough pressure to slice the tender flesh of Scott's neck. Derek seemed mesmerised as he focused at the bright red colour pouring from Scott, spilling onto the white rug. Derek seemed at ease as he slowly removed all of Scott's clothes and wrapped his body in some ready prepared bin bags and blankets. Derek seemed mechanical as he put the blood soaked clothes into another bag and calmly carried Scott into the white van parked a few streets away. Derek was surprised at how much blood needed to be cleaned up, though he knew he had to be thorough before leaving for Ditching.

Derek checked his watch, it was 10.30 pm, and he had plenty of time to phone Kate.

'Hey you,' shouted Kate as she looked at the distant figure. 'What are you doing down there?' As there was no reply Kate decided to walk nearer to see what the man was looking at.

As Kate approached the figure she realised it was Derek. 'Derek, what the hell, what are you look...'

'Shut up bitch,' Derek cut in as he roughly grabbed her arm. Kate could smell the whiskey and stale cigarettes on Derek's breath as he pulled her arm behind her back.

He forced her to look at Scott's lifeless body lying in the freshly dug up ground.

'Derek, what's going on here?' These were Kate's last words as Derek threw her on top of Scott's motionless body.

As Derek continued to shovel the moist soil over them both, he was oblivious to the approaching figure, who had witnessed the whole event.

# Simone Jackson

*We are all writers, and,*
*with some help*
*- all of us -*
*without exception*
*have a great story to tell.*
*Every chapter happy, sad ,*
*exciting moments;*
*we can weave the magic cloth*
*and make those moments work.*

# Excess Baggage

I stepped out of the plane, and smiled - I was at my dream destination – on Golden Sands Beach.

I shook my long dark silky hair and lowered my beautifully made-up eyes as I stepped into the white stretch limo I had booked to take me to the Golden Sands Hotel - no children allowed here - only the mega-rich and famous. This is the life!

Money no object, I wore my Stella McCartney outfit with the knowledge that everyone would be looking at me, my body the envy of most women. Those long hours spent at the gym now seem so worthwhile.

I walk into my hotel, go to my room and open the double doors that lead straight to the Golden Sands beach.

The champagne is waiting, chilling on ice, I smile again to myself; how lucky I am to be here. I can hear my Stuart Weitzman high heeled shoes clicking loudly on the marble floor as I walk across the lounge. I have a ground floor beach fronted suite decorated in lavish white, beige, and gold furnishings. I feel very much at home and start to relax.

I shall have a bath. The bath is surrounded by what must be a hundred lighted candles - heavenly!

I lay my clothes out ready for the party tonight. I put my Clive Christian perfume ($215,000's worth) on my dressing room table and totally chill. Two weeks of bliss. I deserve it – I work hard enough. Now it's ME TIME.

The phone rings – I curse – and switch off my laptop. It's my friend Doris. "What you bin up to Mavis?" She squeals." Not on one of your virtual holidays again! One day you'll stay out there and never come back!!"

I wish, I thought, I wish...

# Stella Goorney

*In the past I have been an actress, potter and theatre critic, though not all at the same time! However I have now settled down to writing occasional poetry and short stories, some of which have ended up on Radio 4.*

Stella Goorney

## Better Off

I used to know every stone
of the street, every crack,
and the way the puddles looked
rainbow coloured, in a certain light.

Sent out from the clock-ticking
dimness of cluttered kitchens,
Full of washing and rag rugs,
We would play on the loud
hop-scotching pavement, cheerful
and in the swim (one knicker leg
worn down this season),
with chapped hands, skinned knees,
picked noses, skipping, playing marbles
or sometimes flailing on roller skates.

As though we owned the place.

Quite different then on the new estate
where all was ordered neat and quiet.
Front doors shut for privacy,
houses set back from vulgar roads.
Just eyes alive, watchful  behind
net curtains, tastefully arranged.

It was all planned
and we should have been glad
because we had bettered ourselves
Into the land of the indoor loo
and constant hot running.

But how we mourned behind our veils of net
for the noise and clamour
as we gazed at the desolating street.

Stella Goorney

# Back Street Venice

The canal only knows
the back side of a town.
Knows its rear walls,
their lines of rubbish bags
slumped like seals basking.

For the sharp faced dwellers
on twilight edges,
and no-hopers
its tideless torpor
and balding towpath
are their wildlife.
For pinched and lonely truants,
their away-day of discovery.

It receives the skeletons of prams
and small mammals. Holds them,
 sometimes turbid,
secret as burial,
sometimes limpid
as through a window.

Is ritually dragged
at every Disappearance.

Further on, in country mood,
is bright with families
in yachting caps.
But, though lean and linear,
child of geometry and ruler,
this delinquent will never go straight.

Suffering the blooding of sunset
down its long pale gleam,
which nightfall leaves till last
then covers brusquely,
it becomes the haunt
of the up to no good,
lovers, the homeless, the insane.

# Stella Goorney

## Dying Day

The old woman quickens her pace
through the winter afternoon,
breathes shallowly against the cold,
with bronchial sounds and hesitations.

"Help the Aged" the sign exhorts
the passer by. Or perhaps warns:
"Help! The Aged!"
The woman stops suspicious
as a horse at the door of
the knacker's van. "Just passing"
her manner conveys.
"I don't belong here, never,
not in a day centre,
for the aged"

But the warmth inside is close
and murmurous as a bee hive,
sagacious and dense
with its accumulated pasts.

The massed presence of old age
keeps the future at bay.
Time dare not come in.
Outside it whizzes by
street corners aflicker with the
restless flamboyant young,
and the day, bored with its own greyness,
yawns cavernous, and brings on
a premature night.

# Charity Begins At Home

I can sound very plausible. Can sound 'well spoken' as they say. It's the drink that lands you on the streets, not lack of education.

So I go into one of the big offices round here and explain, to this smarty-boots manager, that I'm collecting for Oxfam. 'I'm just on my lunch break,' I say. I'm all kitted out with a clean enough suit – got in the Oxfam shop, funnily enough – and the proper Oxfam tin. Oh they're easy to mock-up. I'm a dab hand. So I suggest perhaps I could go round his office? Whatever anyone would like to give?

He buys it! 'Of course, dear fellow' he says airily.

I get a good haul.

Later, a bit flushed by success, on a bit of a high, I have to admit, I decide to fit in some begging, but with a different persona this time (whiney, cockney and shabbier). A punter bends to drop a coin. Our eyes meet. It's my smarty-boots friend!

'I never forget a face' he says, very softly.

Stella Goorney

# Curtains For Arthur

Arthur planned to invite Evie for a drink after the show. He rather fancied he was in with a chance there, though he realised he was batting above his league, as his father, a cricketing man, would have put it. Evie was the glamorous leading lady and Arthur was a mere novice in the company, playing his first major role. Up till then it had been butlers or victims who got murdered in the first scene.

Arthur, however, was an eternal optimist and waited for his entrance, with hope in his heart, confident that he would wow the audience and dazzle Evie with his command of the scene. Meanwhile, waiting for his cue, he tried the door handle – just to check. But – oh horrors – it seemed to be stuck! He cursed the incompetent stage carpenter. In seconds he was to make his entrance through this very door and declare himself as the illicit lover of the woman now on stage.

Gerald, playing her wronged husband, finished his speech with a flourish and Arthur's cue came. Silence.

Evie, playing the adulterous wife, fidgeted and tried a little ad lib. Arthur, in the wings, sweating and desperate, didn't know what to do. The audience grew restive. Finally, in total panic, he put his shoulder to the door and heaved. The door gave! But unfortunately, the whole of the wall with it, revealing the cavernous backstage and two surprised scene shifters on a break.

He sidled thorough the gap between scenery and proscenium arch, pushed the wall back and leant on it for mutual support. Some pictures had clattered to the ground, he saw, but not the grandfather clock which, fortunately, was painted on. Gerald looked aghast. Evie turned upstage and directed upon Arthur a look of naked hatred. As though it were his fault!

He also detected waves of disapproval from the audience. Though this was understandable. Here was a man who had not only stolen the hero's wife, but also pulled down her wall!

He gabbled though his speech without recourse to expression, looked round wildly, and exited – through the fireplace! This feat achieved a round of applause.

However there was nothing for it now but to ring down the curtain.

# Final Draft

Gordon was in the throes of creativity. A word escaped him. He searched for it. But then characters began to escape. This was supposed to be Science Fiction, but really! They were manifesting as voices and actually had the effrontery to speak words – which Gordon was pretty sure he hadn't even written.

One of them, it appeared, was called Auger. 'We are gravely concerned with the way you Humanoids are comporting yourselves' Auger intoned. 'We feel bound to warn you about this.'

'WHAT?' Gordon forgot about the word he was searching for, and searched for others, ones denoting shock and outrage.

Auger didn't seem to notice. He proceeded smoothly; 'Well we feel, to a certain extent, responsible. You are, after all, one of our colonies …'

'What rubbish! I'm not having you say that.' Gordon had found the words.

'You mean you didn't realise you were a colony?'

This idea was received with merriment amongst Auger's friends.

Gordon grew red with indignation. This wasn't the way his novel was supposed to go at all.

'This is a mess!' he cried. 'I shall have to start all over again. In fact what I should do is simply hit the 'delete' button. I've a good mind to.'

This provoked more merriment.

That did it!

'Stop!' But already Auger's voice was beginning to sound faint and far away.

'You silly Humanoid! You've just deleted yourself!'

# Tim Shelton-Jones

*I was happily adjusting to life without
computer programming, scouring the
forgotten corners of time for mutant
forms of poetry and philosophy, when
one day along came the marvel
of grandparenthood. None of this made
any difference though to my 26-year-
long dedication to NightWriters.
The End (not).*

Tim Shelton-Jones

# Because, one morning

Today, the sky makes itself blue
Because it can.
If Claire laughs, or groans in horror,
It is because her head is in another world
That writes itself from the pages of a book.
The plumbing hums through gritted joints
Because life in a tight pipe is so very pressured.
And birds sing because they want to paint the air with many colours
Bright as the trees and the flowers
And the pearly shades of rain -
Or just because they want to
Or just because.
Meanwhile...
The morning pours in through my eyes, my ears,
It is inspired, it has the right to be everywhere,
The dream-places are flooding with light
And my mind waits for something to happen in it
Because that way it will know what to do when the time comes.
I am filling up slowly -
A soft old engine waiting to go,
Waiting for my own 'because'.

# Criminals in the Wood

Here is the place
We once set fire to each other. No-one saw. Over there
In that clearing behind the patch of brambles
We were robbers. I stole the breath, the senses, out of you.
You stole them back, and more - all my lovely loot. We never told.
Later,
Down behind the big old oak,
I swindled and cheated my way into your private treasure store,
Eyed the glittering rubies, the snowy pearls
With full intent; you took your revenge -
No breaking and entering, no axe,
Just a neat line in chat round by the back door:
There were my bullion bars, never seen before. Ransacked,
I gave up, made peace,
We concealed our crimes under a mouldering leaf
Then tried each other - Verdict: Guilty, both -
But of diminished responsibility
Being mere adults at the time. Today,
We stroll through shocks of silly daffodils,
Their ashen mouths hang open, trying to say 'We know!'
We silence them with smiles,
Our hands discovering through touch
The sweet unholy suck of secrecy:
The memories of deeds that made us us.

Tim Shelton-Jones

# Earth Angel

An angel got lost
On its way back to heaven.
There it was, sat on our roof
Crying: a slow, shivering sound
Like harps drowning.
So we let it in.
All white it stood - soft marble
And fluttering translucent wings,
Its toes bluish on the cold kitchen floor.
It asked for honey and cream,
Then told us it had been sent down to guide some infant,
Already tired of life,
Into the hands of waiting great-aunts and uncles,
Grandmothers, far-distant cousins.  So many hands...
The little creature looked up at us
With eyes of sky-blue,
Its face round as a new moon.
And a tear like a shooting star
Sped over that smooth alabaster cheek.
The dimensions that lead up to heaven
Are dying, it said.
Earth is breaking away, falling into itself,
The sky cannot hold it
So heavy the world is now,
A black-hole of sin.  We nodded,
Knowing that weight within us.
So we made a little tea
And sang some songs together.  When it died,
We took it to the garden and found a home for it
Beneath the apple trees.
How rosy and round the fruit were that year,

Shining a little by night, like a skyful of comets.
One bite each we had, but so strong was the taste
The rest went to the birds,
Who sang the red twilight through
As though the dark would never come.

# Help!

Autumn
Bright
Cold
Decay
Rain
Nights
Coats
Blankets
Bonfires
Smoke
Apples
Windfalls
Gales
Umbrellas
Storm
Help!
Fear
Winter
Ice
Time
Eternity
White
Death
Help!
Spirits
Shadows
Dreams
Help!
Cocoon
Dawn
Spring
Newborn
Hunger
Cry
Help!

# Out of the Forest

Remember, back in the old days, we ran wild -
Legs kicking out, and sticking our wet snouts into everything,
We rootled where we pleased
Trampling over the woods, grunting and snorting,
Fighting - was it with friend or foe? - we didn't care
As we chased red-eyed after the ladies. Oh those nights out in the
rain
Paralysed by lightning; and the wolves high on hunger, ready for us.
Midwinter, skidding on night ice and lost amongst the odourless
snow,
Our insides burning on empty,
We'd wake blinded, the sun erupting from storm clouds
And coming at us through the frost-hardened forest,
Every tree evil with ice
Grabbing and stabbing at us.

Or else, dreaming the summer days through – remember?
We laid ourselves out then on the warm rocks at noon
And sunk like truffles into the earth of our piggy souls.

Today
We inhabit a box, with a yard of grass,
Are fed scraps through bars,
Can't even dirty our straw properly. We see only straight lines,
Feel no wind; smell no fear.  Scratching at nothing
I peer down at the tall ones through my useless tusks,
And grunt.
They love it.

Tim Shelton-Jones

# In Praise of Pudding

O Pudding, Pudding, rich and round!
Custards and Sauces!  Silver spoons!
And Baked Apples, and Pastries all a-crumble-o!

The sun sinks down in the December sky,
And snorings tremble from beside the fire.
The dog looks up with an imploring eye -
What is this marvel, this solemn, secret bliss
Of humankind?   All wreathed in steam!
O brown-skinned, creamy, pulpy Rice!
And Raspberry Tartlets, sugared a-lightly-o.
Ye generous Jellies!  We are quite overcome
By your serenades of scent, your gay parade
Of form and hue  - bless-ed as the flowers
Of summer you are.  O Patient Pudding!  Yes, so very true,
And waiting till the last  - so sure of victr'y, you overwhelm
With kindly strike of taste and flavour.  Slaves forever at your table,
We serve; you minister.  O proud crusts, rising full; and yielding,
Warmly, as a matron's flesh.  Yet fair you are too,
And tender - as new life lying cool
Upon the palsied senses of our years.
Polite, personable and profound -
Ever you speak to us of inner joys.

The door swings closed now;
Guests are departed, content
And strolling 'neath the stars
As the first few flakes glitter into midnight -
Nature's own sweet icing, dusting the frost-hard land.  Indoors,
The perfumes of a gracious day
Still linger.
As of good things remembered.
O Pudding, Pudding, burning bright
In the stomach of the night !
What immortal hand or eye
Could bake thy peerless recipe?

Delia Smith?

# Who's Who ?

Who exactly *is* who?
*Why* are they who?
How did they *become* who?
Or did someone make them who?
And, if so,
Who?

What do you have to do
To be someone who's Someone
Who's someone you want to be?
Or do you just become who-
ever you have to be, whether you
want to or not?

And what if you don't like
Who you are?  Can you undo yourself,
Go who-less into the human zoo?

Can someone come along
And un-who you: become you.
And, if they do, would you know,
Could you find out who
They are
And what to do?
There can't be two of you.

And how can I tell
If you are who you say you are?
Or if I am who I think I am
Or just who you say I am;
or else someone who
would like to be someone who-
's a little like me
And a lot like you.

And what are you supposed to do
If you're unique
And none of this applies to you?
I wish I knew.
So,
Please tell me who
Decides who's who.
I've got a question or two.


## Safe Journey


Heading for the car that evening
We retrieved our bags,
And you wished us 'Safe journey home'
As you always did; but this time
Softly
And from your bed.
I, on impulse
Murmured 'You too',
Though we all knew you were going nowhere -
No place, that is,
Where we might follow.

Tim Shelton-Jones

# Scene on the Train to London

He's a nice guy
But she deserves better.
Whole symphonies of silence pass between them,
Her face lit from within
By thought, or music, or some fiery place.
Ages pass behind her eyes, whole galaxies collide there.
His face though is a puzzle straining to solve itself,
Like a bucket stuck halfway down a well
Twisting towards freedom.

But when they talk
The bald red globe of a December sun
Falling through towers into the sleepy Thames
Fires their eyes with wonder warmed to love.
Their smiles touch, and I wonder:
Can it last ?

# To do list

Mend our fences
Remember my manners
Read your mind
Stay kind.
Write something wonderful
Outshine youth
Look into the mirror
Face truth.

Made in the USA
Charleston, SC
08 October 2015